Billy & Buddy

Roba

REMEMBER THIS, BUDDY?

9th CINEBOOK
The 9th Art Publisher

Original title: Boule & Bill 6 – Tu te rappelles, Bill ?

Original edition: © Studio Boule & Bill, 2008
by Roba

English translation: © 2009 Cinebook Ltd

Translator: Luke Spear
Lettering and text layout: Imadjinn
Printed in Spain by Just Colour Graphic

This edition first published in Great Britain in 2009 by
Cinebook Ltd
56 Beech Avenue
Canterbury, Kent
CT4 7TA
www.cinebook.com

A CIP catalogue record for this book
is available from the British Library

ISBN 978-1-905460-91-5

Long Live the Tide!

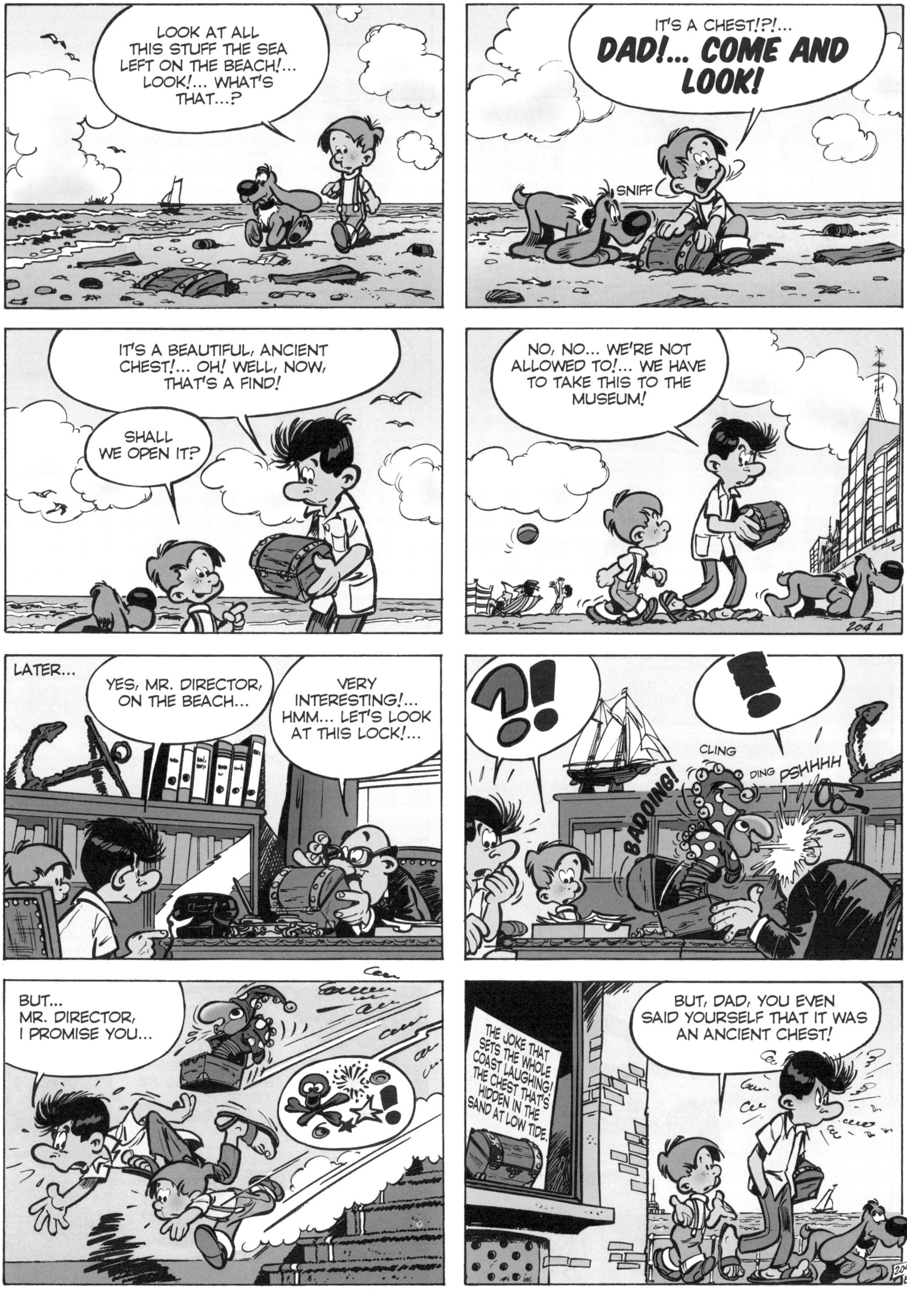
LOOK AT ALL THIS STUFF THE SEA LEFT ON THE BEACH!... LOOK!... WHAT'S THAT...?
IT'S A CHEST!?!...
DAD!... COME AND LOOK!
SNIFF
IT'S A BEAUTIFUL, ANCIENT CHEST!... OH! WELL, NOW, THAT'S A FIND!
SHALL WE OPEN IT?
NO, NO... WE'RE NOT ALLOWED TO!... WE HAVE TO TAKE THIS TO THE MUSEUM!
LATER...
YES, MR. DIRECTOR, ON THE BEACH...
VERY INTERESTING!... HMM... LET'S LOOK AT THIS LOCK!...
?!
!
CLING
DING
PSHHHH
BADOING!
BUT... MR. DIRECTOR, I PROMISE YOU...
THE JOKE THAT SETS THE WHOLE COAST LAUGHING! THE CHEST THAT'S HIDDEN IN THE SAND AT LOW TIDE.
BUT, DAD, YOU EVEN SAID YOURSELF THAT IT WAS AN ANCIENT CHEST!

Farsighted

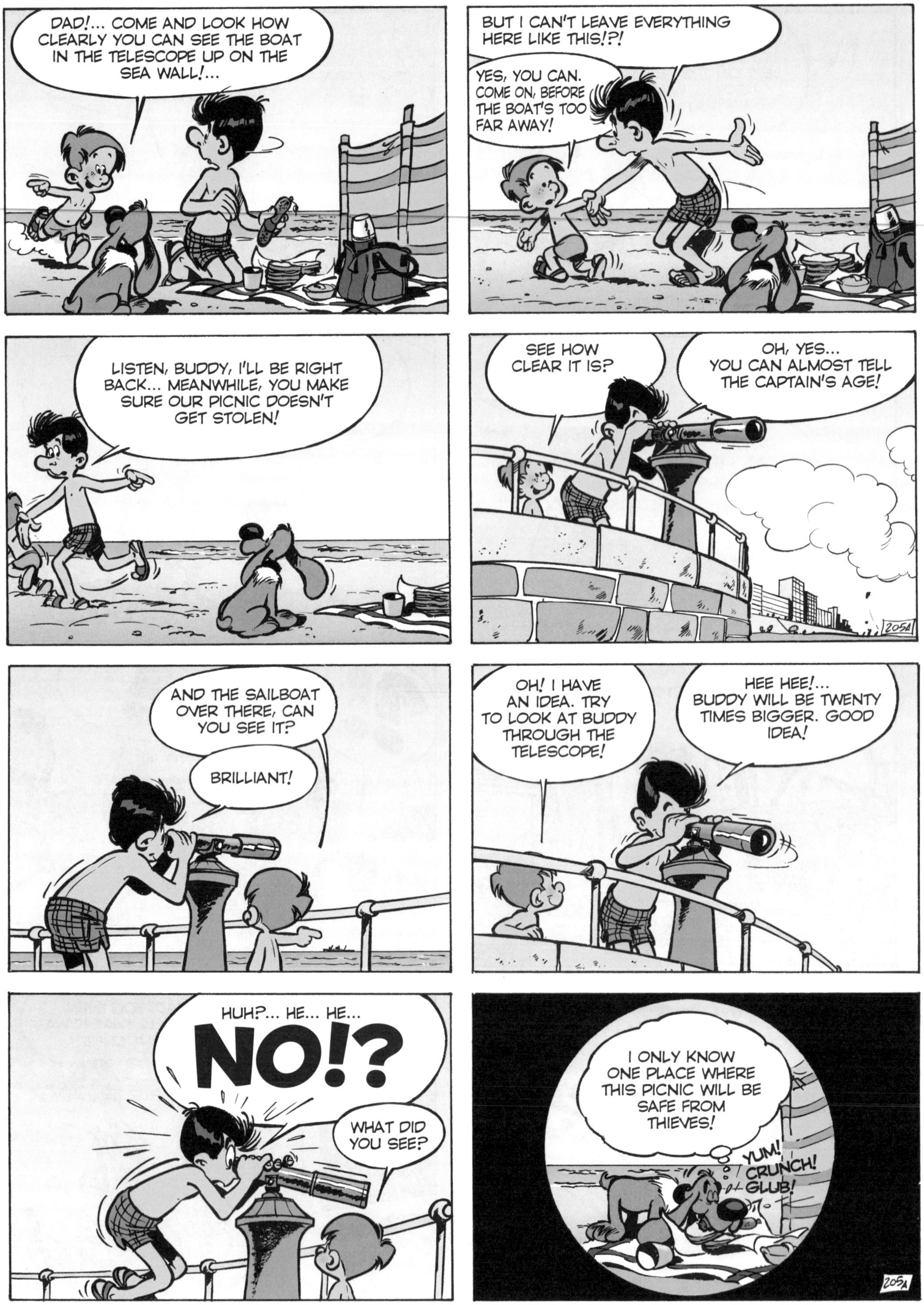
DAD!... COME AND LOOK HOW CLEARLY YOU CAN SEE THE BOAT IN THE TELESCOPE UP ON THE SEA WALL!...
BUT I CAN'T LEAVE EVERYTHING HERE LIKE THIS!?!
YES, YOU CAN. COME ON, BEFORE THE BOAT'S TOO FAR AWAY!
LISTEN, BUDDY, I'LL BE RIGHT BACK... MEANWHILE, YOU MAKE SURE OUR PICNIC DOESN'T GET STOLEN!
SEE HOW CLEAR IT IS?
OH, YES... YOU CAN ALMOST TELL THE CAPTAIN'S AGE!
AND THE SAILBOAT OVER THERE, CAN YOU SEE IT?
BRILLIANT!
OH! I HAVE AN IDEA. TRY TO LOOK AT BUDDY THROUGH THE TELESCOPE!
HEE HEE!... BUDDY WILL BE TWENTY TIMES BIGGER. GOOD IDEA!
HUH?... HE... HE...
NO!?
WHAT DID YOU SEE?
I ONLY KNOW ONE PLACE WHERE THIS PICNIC WILL BE SAFE FROM THIEVES!
YUM!
CRUNCH!
GLUB!

Post-relaxation

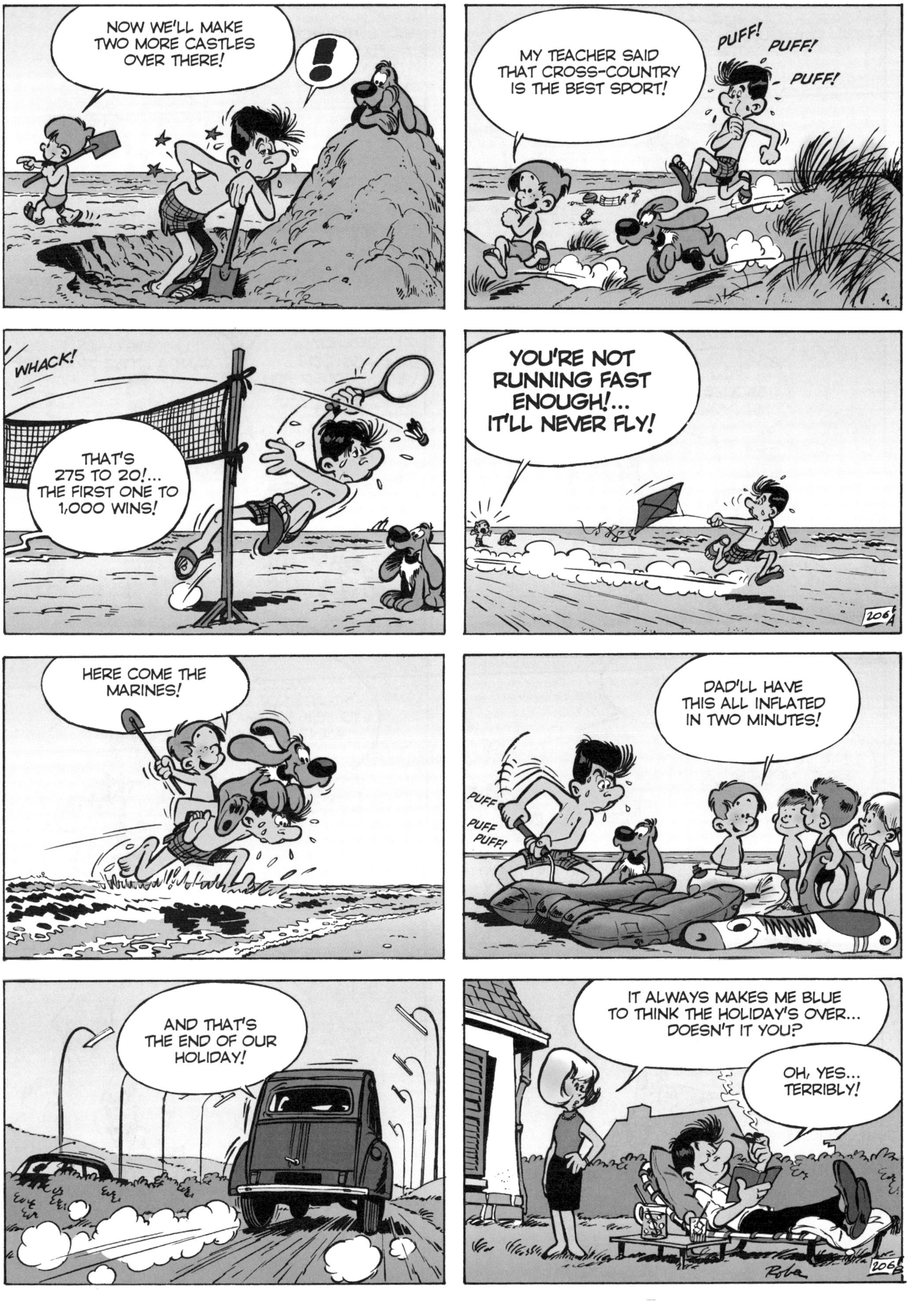
NOW WE'LL MAKE TWO MORE CASTLES OVER THERE!
!
MY TEACHER SAID THAT CROSS-COUNTRY IS THE BEST SPORT!
PUFF! PUFF! PUFF!
WHACK!
THAT'S 275 TO 20!... THE FIRST ONE TO 1,000 WINS!
YOU'RE NOT RUNNING FAST ENOUGH!... IT'LL NEVER FLY!
HERE COME THE MARINES!
DAD'LL HAVE THIS ALL INFLATED IN TWO MINUTES!
PUFF PUFF PUFF!
AND THAT'S THE END OF OUR HOLIDAY!
IT ALWAYS MAKES ME BLUE TO THINK THE HOLIDAY'S OVER... DOESN'T IT YOU?
OH, YES... TERRIBLY!
Roba

Hu-Morris

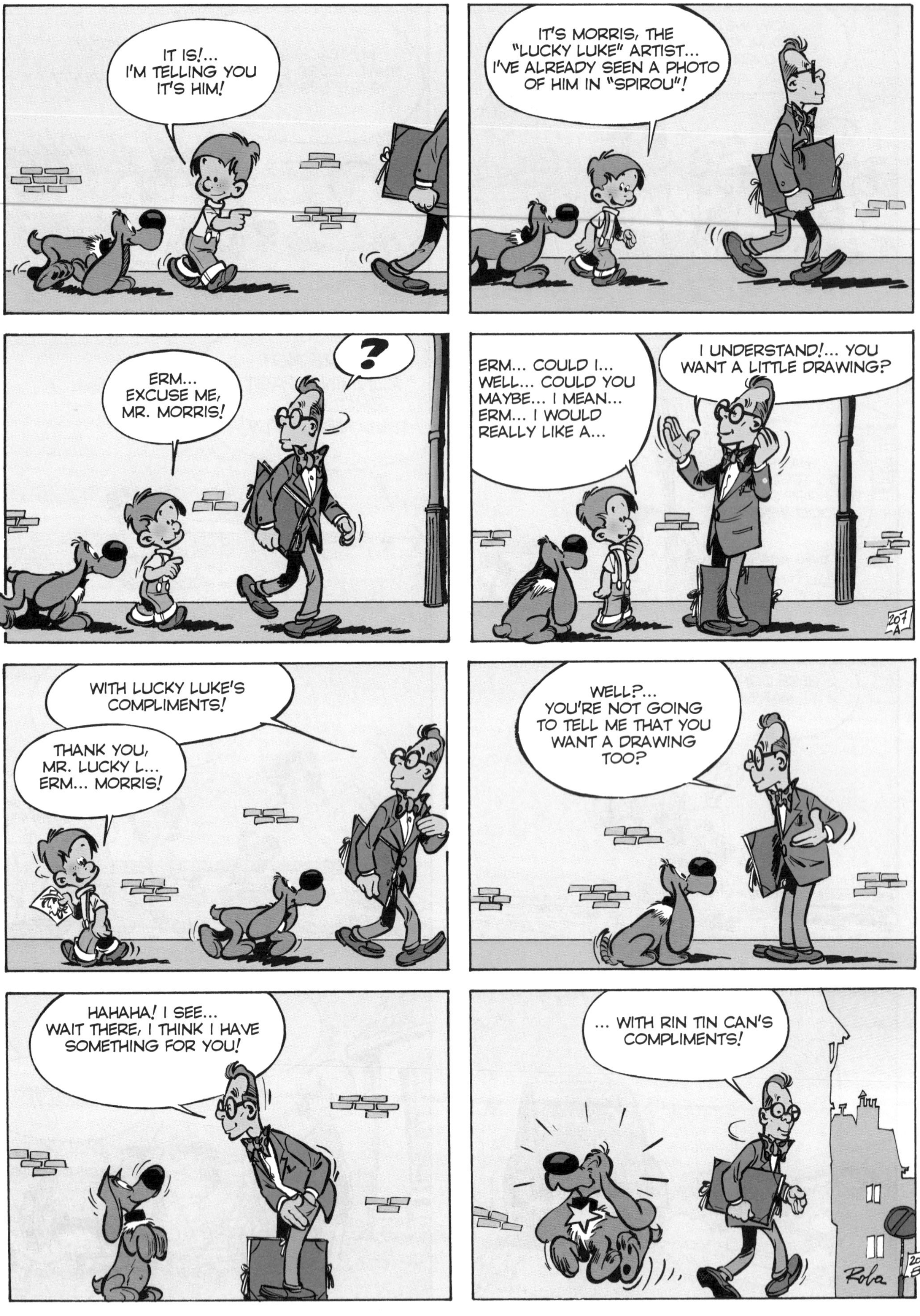
IT IS!... I'M TELLING YOU IT'S HIM!
IT'S MORRIS, THE "LUCKY LUKE" ARTIST... I'VE ALREADY SEEN A PHOTO OF HIM IN "SPIROU"!
ERM... EXCUSE ME, MR. MORRIS!
?
ERM... COULD I... WELL... COULD YOU MAYBE... I MEAN... ERM... I WOULD REALLY LIKE A...
I UNDERSTAND!... YOU WANT A LITTLE DRAWING?
207 A
WITH LUCKY LUKE'S COMPLIMENTS!
THANK YOU, MR. LUCKY L... ERM... MORRIS!
WELL?... YOU'RE NOT GOING TO TELL ME THAT YOU WANT A DRAWING TOO?
HAHAHA! I SEE... WAIT THERE, I THINK I HAVE SOMETHING FOR YOU!
... WITH RIN TIN CAN'S COMPLIMENTS!
Roba
207 B

Sidewalk Sweeper

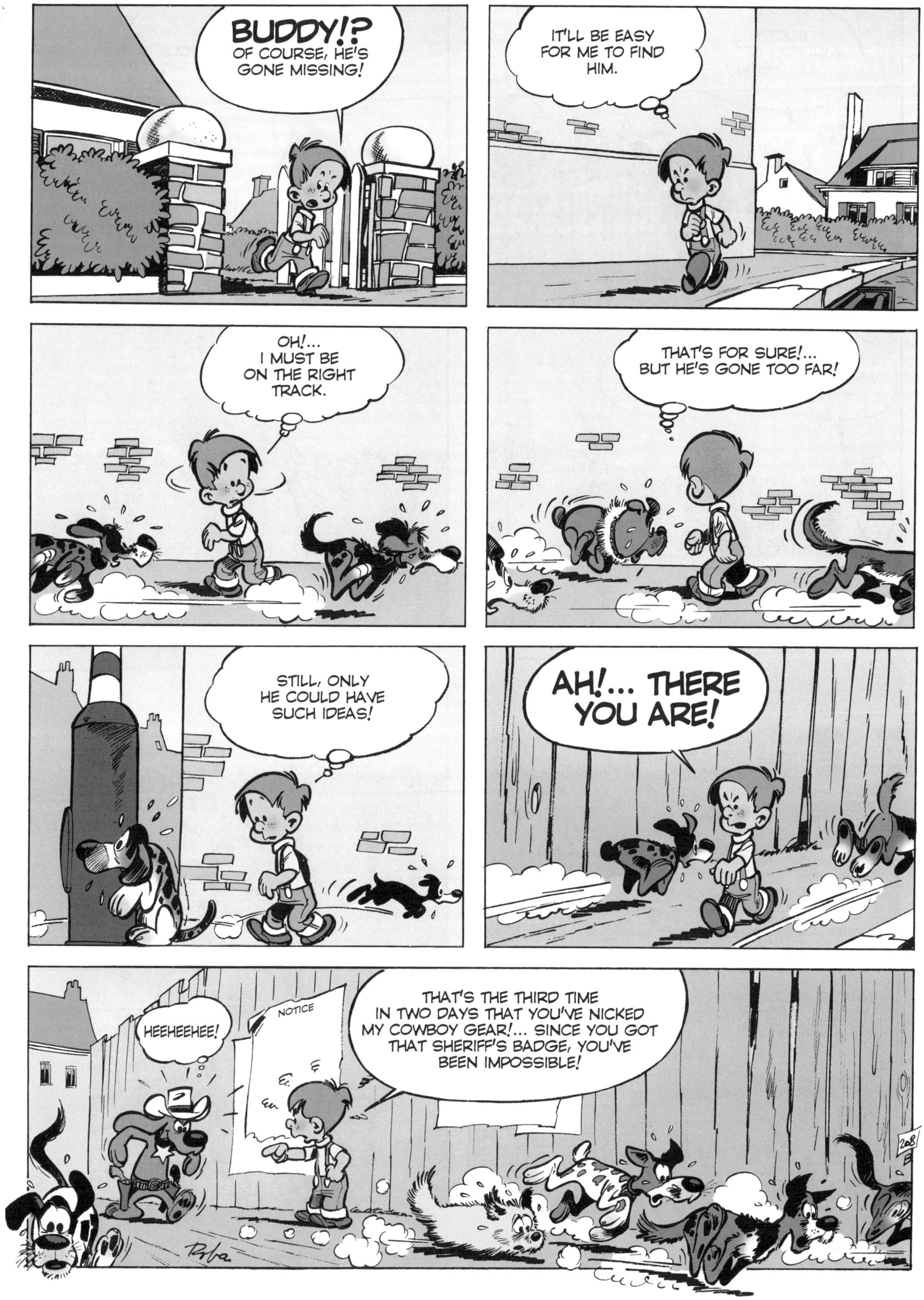

BUDDY!? OF COURSE, HE'S GONE MISSING!
IT'LL BE EASY FOR ME TO FIND HIM.
OH!... I MUST BE ON THE RIGHT TRACK.
THAT'S FOR SURE!... BUT HE'S GONE TOO FAR!
STILL, ONLY HE COULD HAVE SUCH IDEAS!
AH!... THERE YOU ARE!
HEEHEEHEE!
NOTICE
THAT'S THE THIRD TIME IN TWO DAYS THAT YOU'VE NICKED MY COWBOY GEAR!... SINCE YOU GOT THAT SHERIFF'S BADGE, YOU'VE BEEN IMPOSSIBLE!

Binning to Win

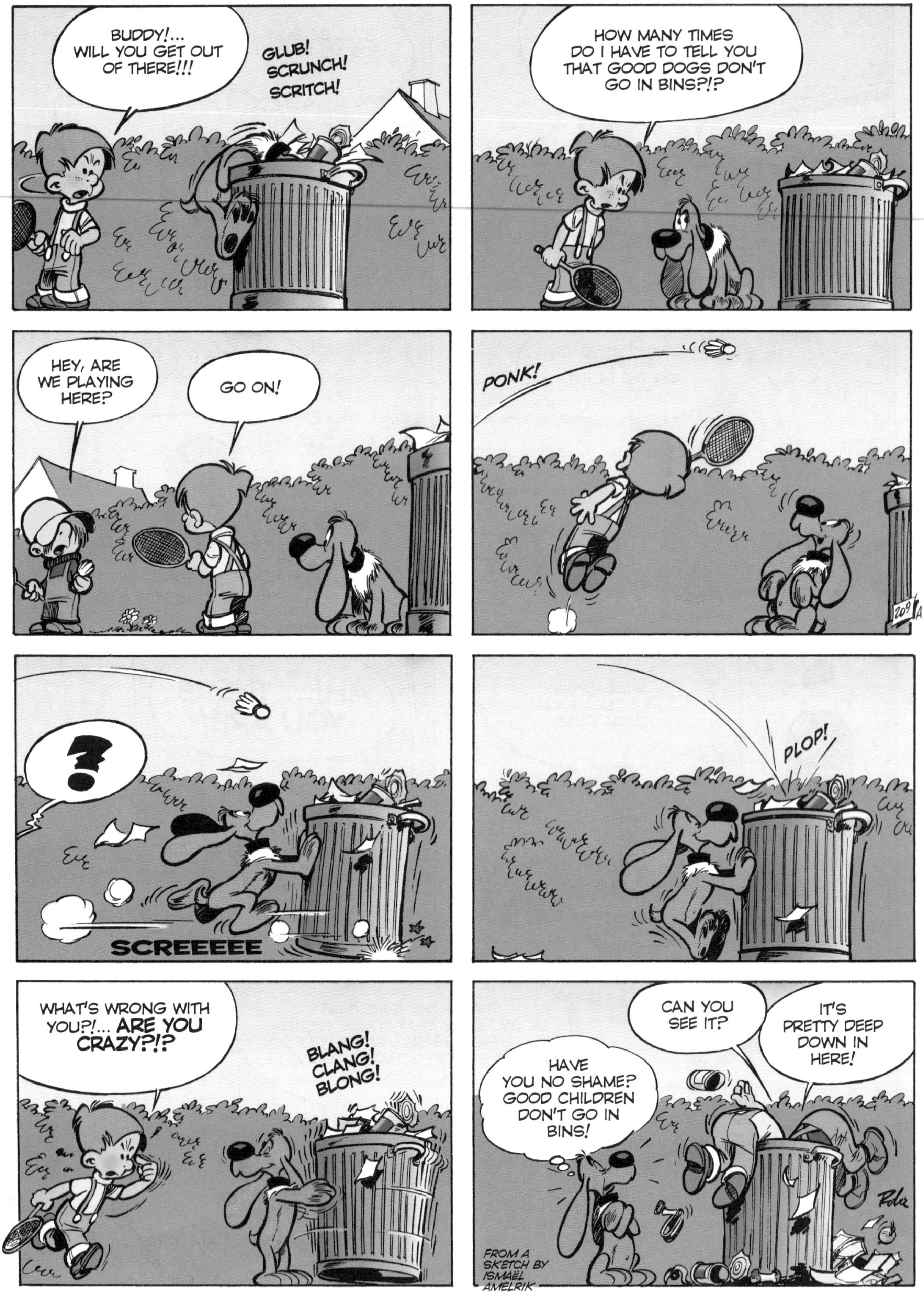
BUDDY!... WILL YOU GET OUT OF THERE!!!
GLUB! SCRUNCH! SCRITCH!
HOW MANY TIMES DO I HAVE TO TELL YOU THAT GOOD DOGS DON'T GO IN BINS?!?
HEY, ARE WE PLAYING HERE?
GO ON!
PONK!
?
SCREEEEE
PLOP!
WHAT'S WRONG WITH YOU?!... ARE YOU CRAZY?!?
BLANG! CLANG! BLONG!
CAN YOU SEE IT?
IT'S PRETTY DEEP DOWN IN HERE!
HAVE YOU NO SHAME? GOOD CHILDREN DON'T GO IN BINS!
FROM A SKETCH BY ISMAËL AMELRIK

Decision-making

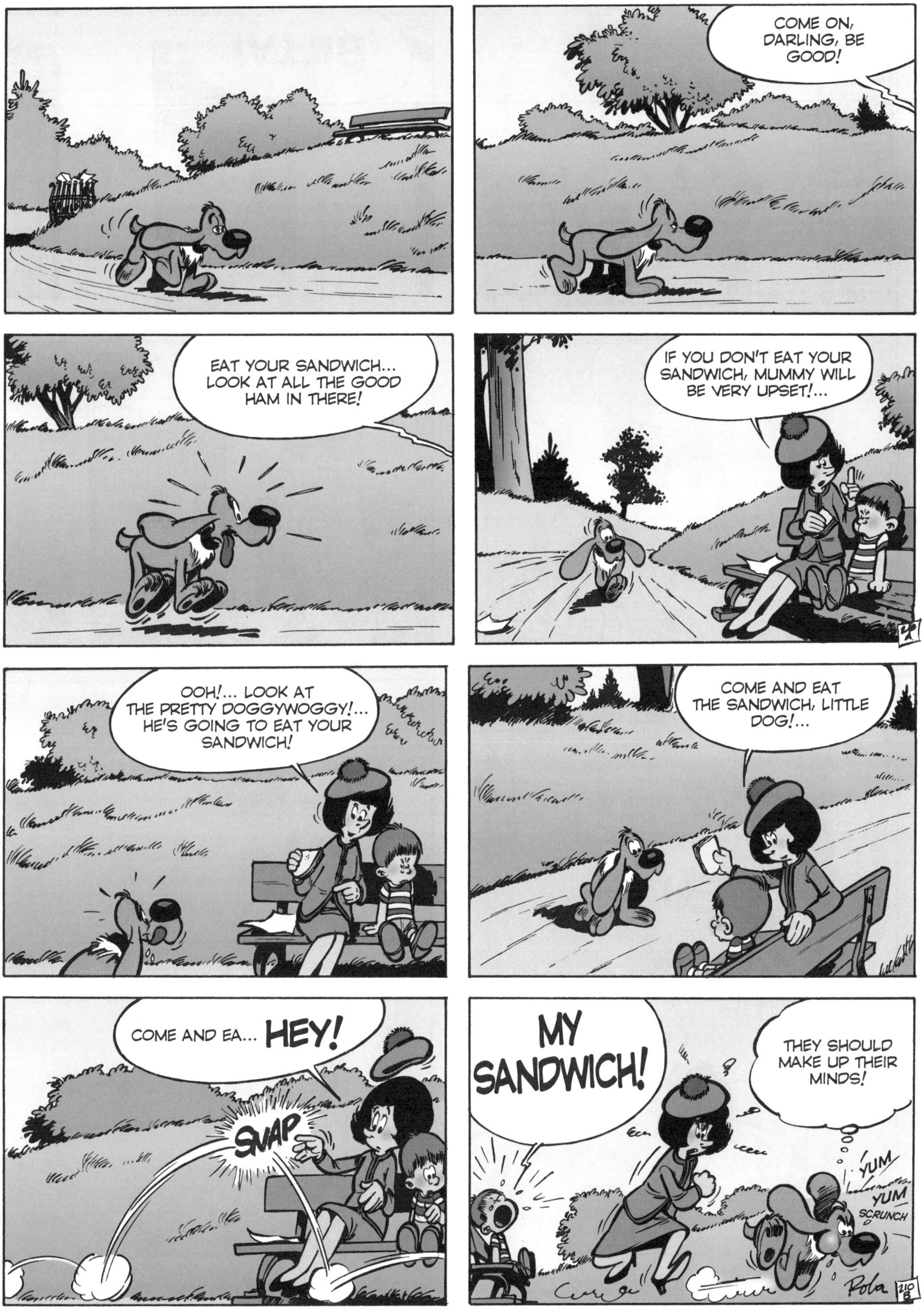
COME ON, DARLING, BE GOOD!
EAT YOUR SANDWICH... LOOK AT ALL THE GOOD HAM IN THERE!
IF YOU DON'T EAT YOUR SANDWICH, MUMMY WILL BE VERY UPSET!...
OOH!... LOOK AT THE PRETTY DOGGYWOGGY!... HE'S GOING TO EAT YOUR SANDWICH!
COME AND EAT THE SANDWICH, LITTLE DOG!...
COME AND EA... HEY!
SNAP
MY SANDWICH!
THEY SHOULD MAKE UP THEIR MINDS!
YUM
YUM
SCRUNCH
Roba

Like Everygum Else

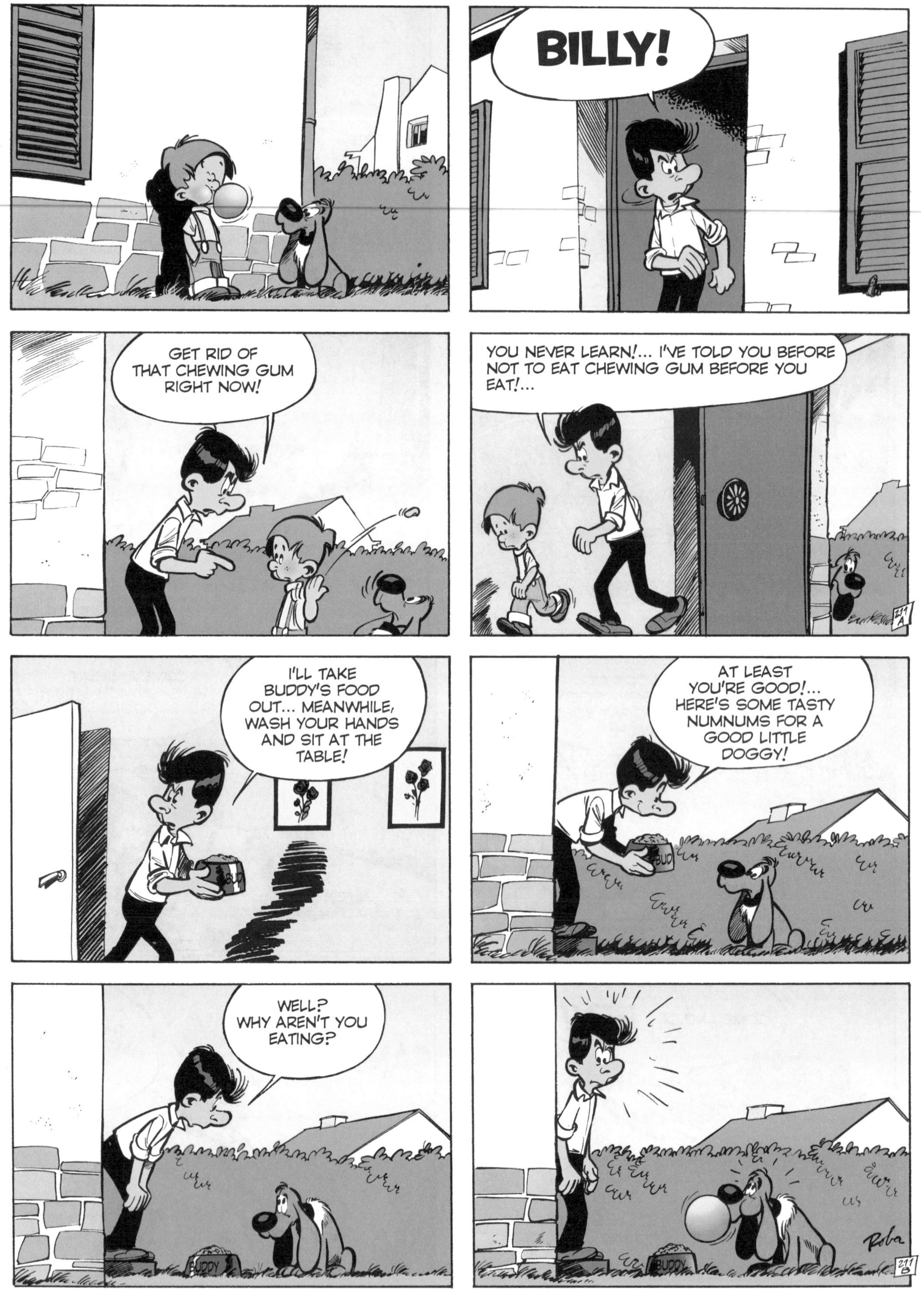
BILLY!
GET RID OF THAT CHEWING GUM RIGHT NOW!
YOU NEVER LEARN!... I'VE TOLD YOU BEFORE NOT TO EAT CHEWING GUM BEFORE YOU EAT!...
I'LL TAKE BUDDY'S FOOD OUT... MEANWHILE, WASH YOUR HANDS AND SIT AT THE TABLE!
AT LEAST YOU'RE GOOD!... HERE'S SOME TASTY NUMNUMS FOR A GOOD LITTLE DOGGY!
WELL? WHY AREN'T YOU EATING?
BUDDY
BUDDY
Roba

Sea Lion, See Lying

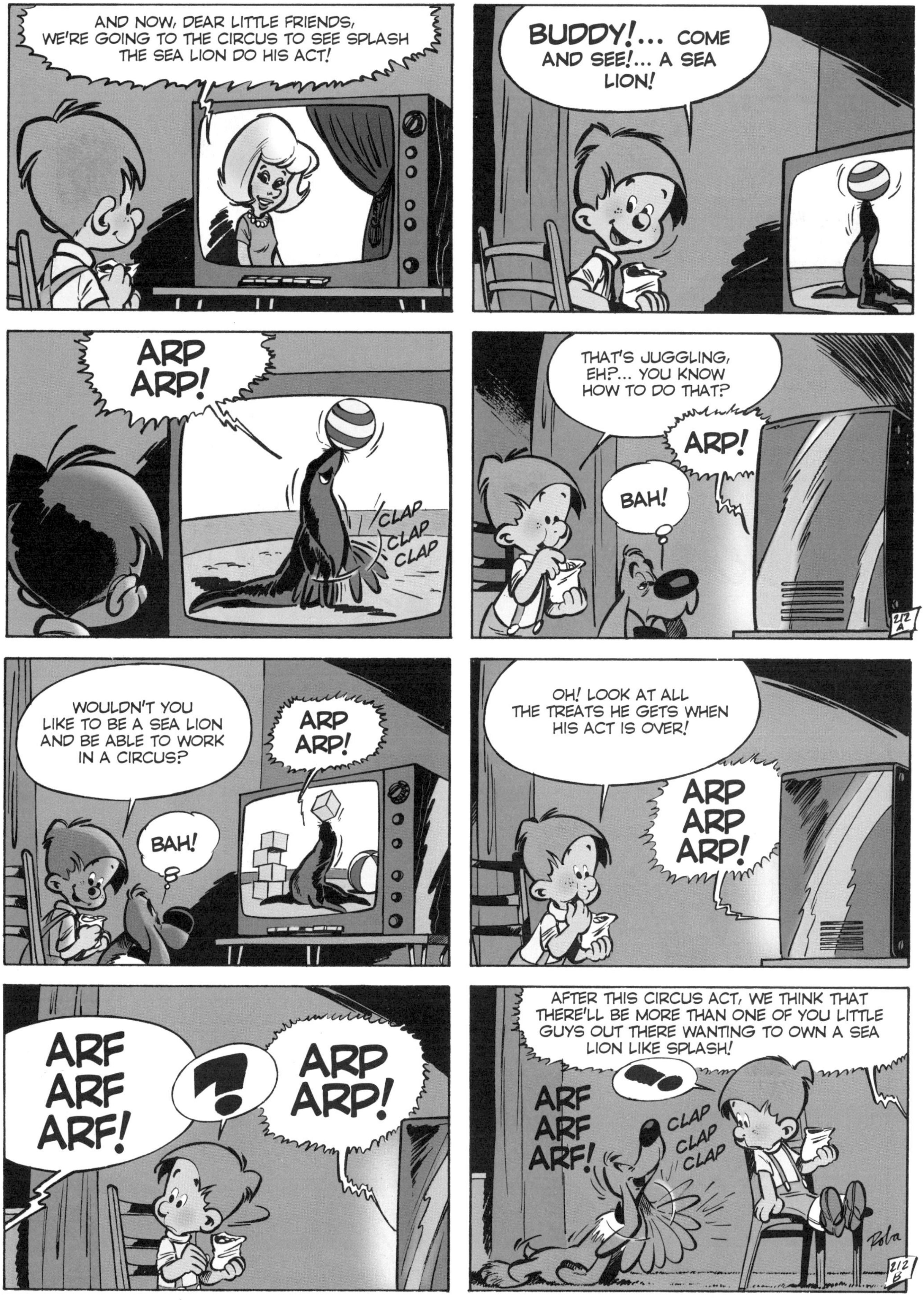
AND NOW, DEAR LITTLE FRIENDS, WE'RE GOING TO THE CIRCUS TO SEE SPLASH THE SEA LION DO HIS ACT!
BUDDY!... COME AND SEE!... A SEA LION!
ARP ARP!
CLAP CLAP CLAP
THAT'S JUGGLING, EH?... YOU KNOW HOW TO DO THAT?
ARP!
BAH!
WOULDN'T YOU LIKE TO BE A SEA LION AND BE ABLE TO WORK IN A CIRCUS?
ARP ARP!
BAH!
OH! LOOK AT ALL THE TREATS HE GETS WHEN HIS ACT IS OVER!
ARP ARP ARP!
ARF ARF ARF!
?
ARP ARP!
AFTER THIS CIRCUS ACT, WE THINK THAT THERE'LL BE MORE THAN ONE OF YOU LITTLE GUYS OUT THERE WANTING TO OWN A SEA LION LIKE SPLASH!
ARF ARF ARF!
CLAP CLAP CLAP
Roba

Haute Cockerture

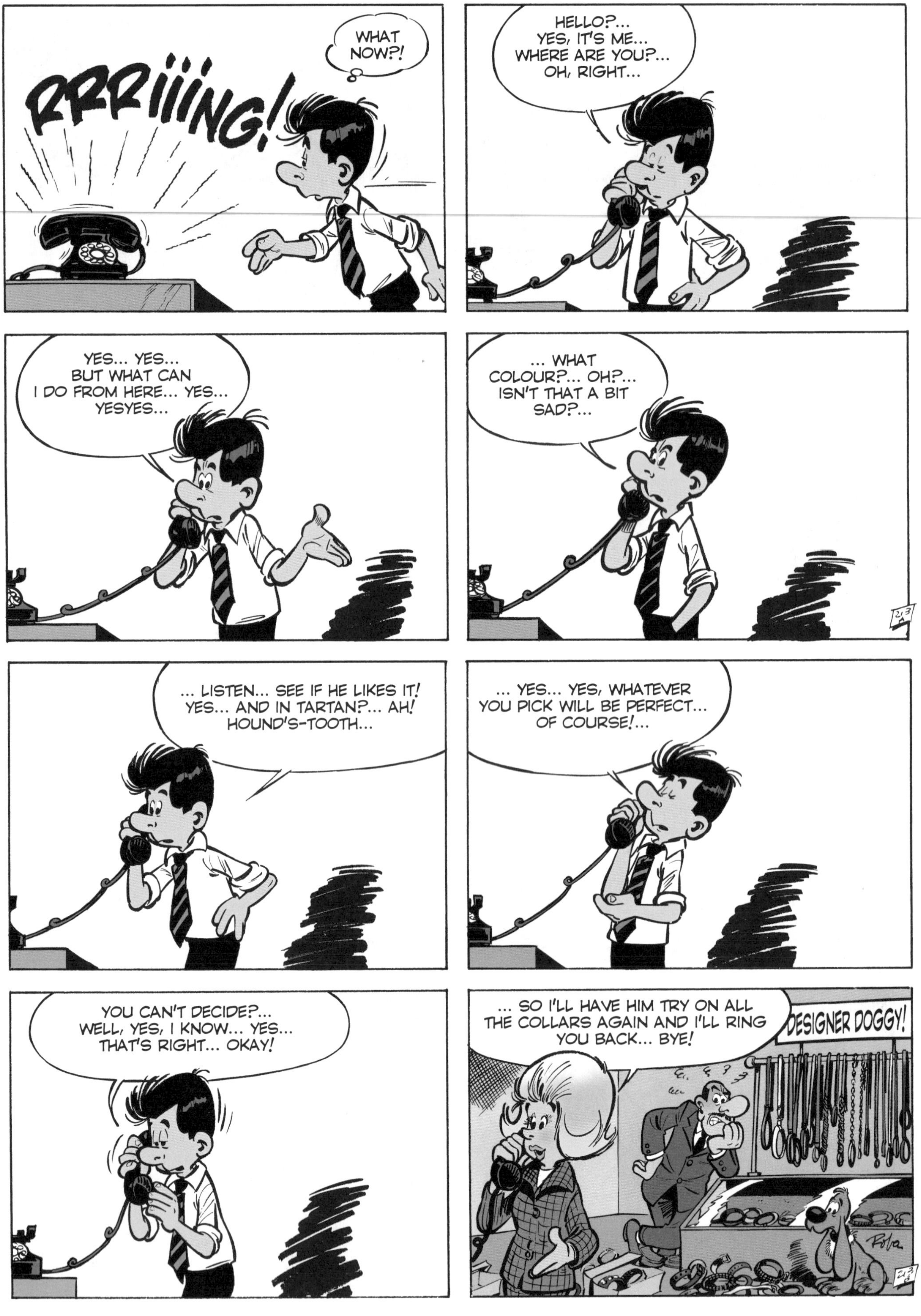
WHAT NOW?!
RRRiiiiNG!
HELLO?... YES, IT'S ME... WHERE ARE YOU?... OH, RIGHT...
YES... YES... BUT WHAT CAN I DO FROM HERE... YES... YESYES...
... WHAT COLOUR?... OH?... ISN'T THAT A BIT SAD?...
... LISTEN... SEE IF HE LIKES IT! YES... AND IN TARTAN?... AH! HOUND'S-TOOTH...
... YES... YES, WHATEVER YOU PICK WILL BE PERFECT... OF COURSE!...
YOU CAN'T DECIDE?... WELL, YES, I KNOW... YES... THAT'S RIGHT... OKAY!
... SO I'LL HAVE HIM TRY ON ALL THE COLLARS AGAIN AND I'LL RING YOU BACK... BYE!
DESIGNER DOGGY!

Flower Power

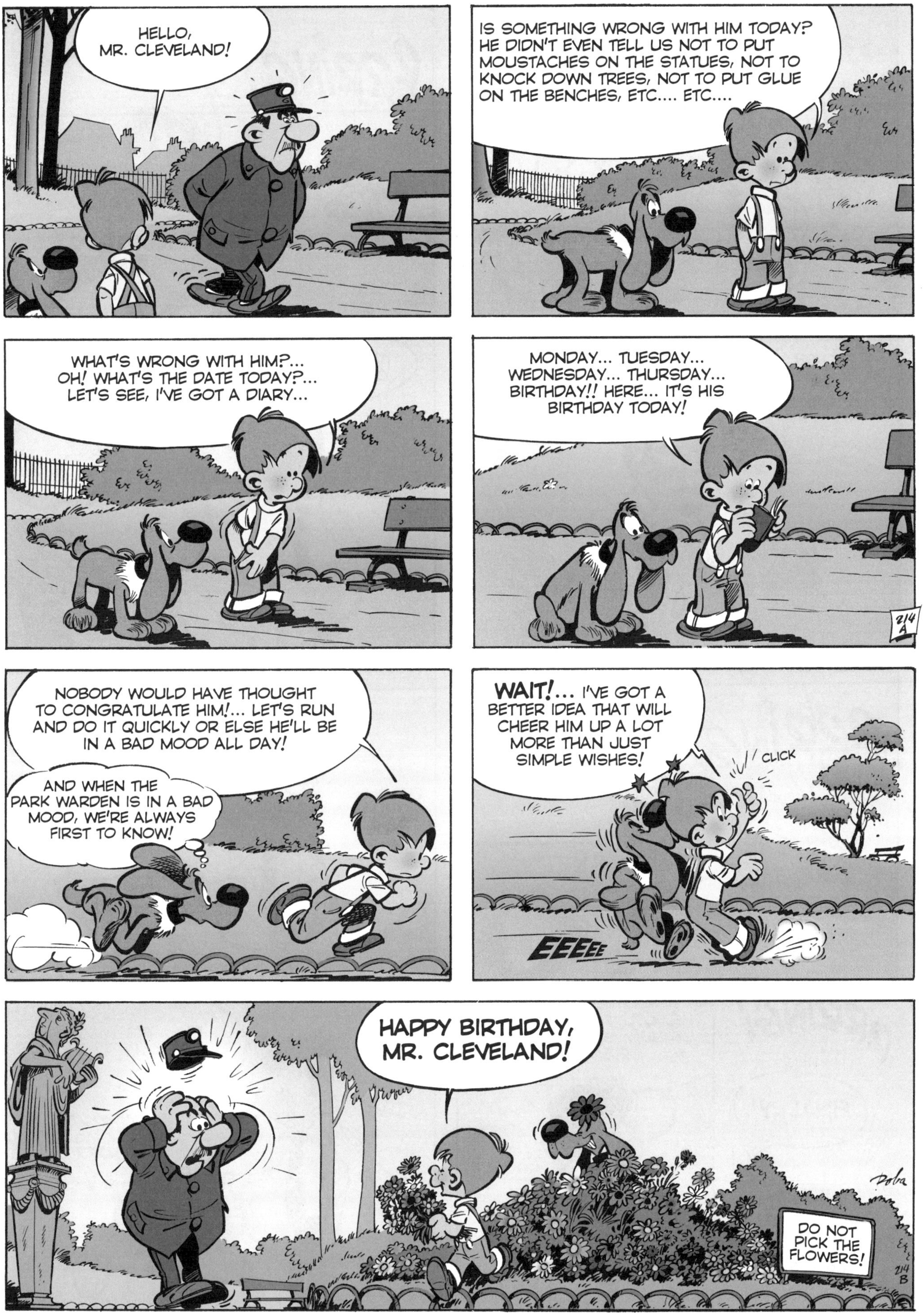
HELLO, MR. CLEVELAND!
IS SOMETHING WRONG WITH HIM TODAY? HE DIDN'T EVEN TELL US NOT TO PUT MOUSTACHES ON THE STATUES, NOT TO KNOCK DOWN TREES, NOT TO PUT GLUE ON THE BENCHES, ETC.... ETC....
WHAT'S WRONG WITH HIM?... OH! WHAT'S THE DATE TODAY?... LET'S SEE, I'VE GOT A DIARY...
MONDAY... TUESDAY... WEDNESDAY... THURSDAY... BIRTHDAY!! HERE... IT'S HIS BIRTHDAY TODAY!
NOBODY WOULD HAVE THOUGHT TO CONGRATULATE HIM!... LET'S RUN AND DO IT QUICKLY OR ELSE HE'LL BE IN A BAD MOOD ALL DAY!
AND WHEN THE PARK WARDEN IS IN A BAD MOOD, WE'RE ALWAYS FIRST TO KNOW!
WAIT!... I'VE GOT A BETTER IDEA THAT WILL CHEER HIM UP A LOT MORE THAN JUST SIMPLE WISHES!
CLICK
EEEEE
HAPPY BIRTHDAY, MR. CLEVELAND!
DO NOT PICK THE FLOWERS!

Have-a-ring-around

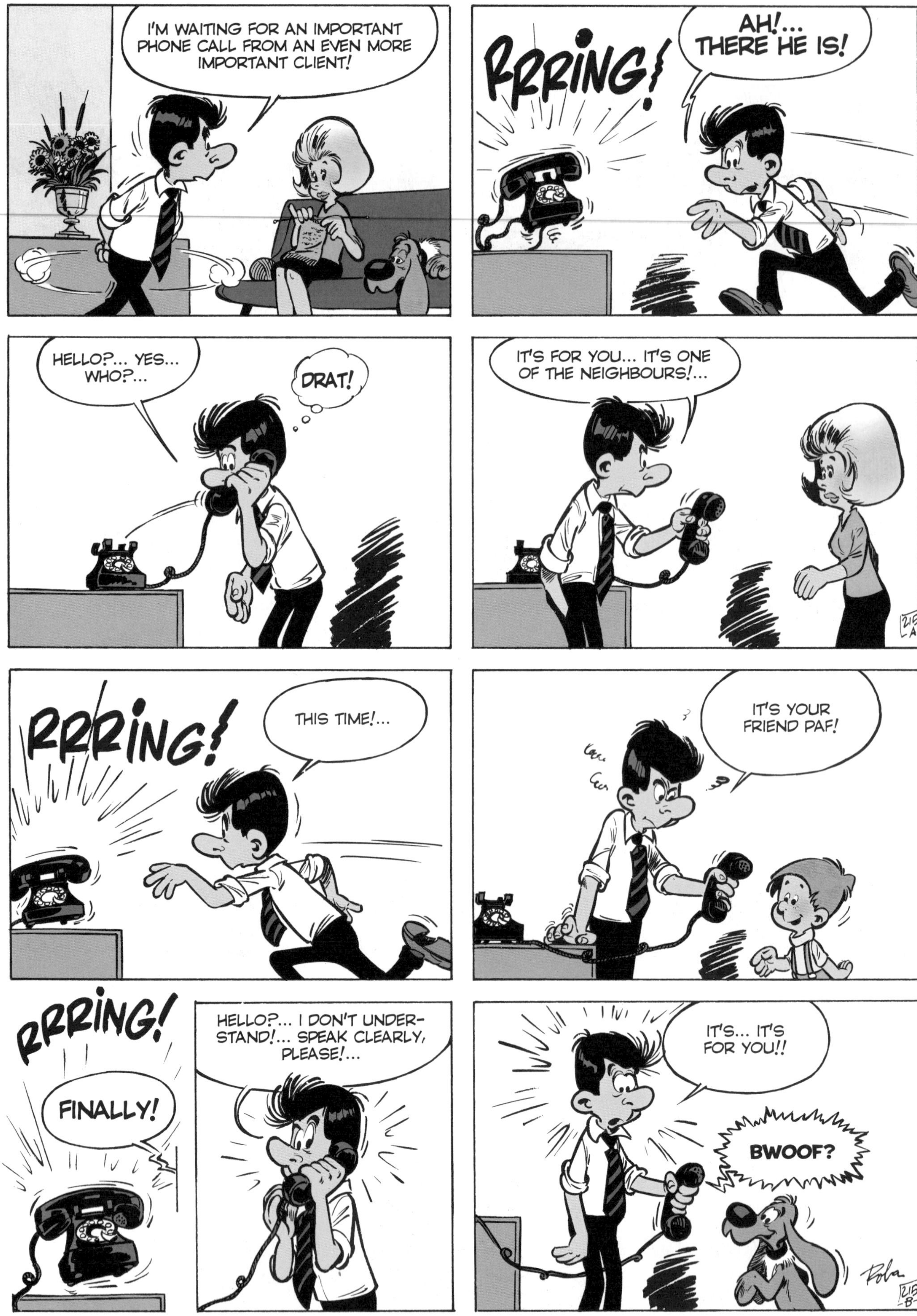
I'M WAITING FOR AN IMPORTANT PHONE CALL FROM AN EVEN MORE IMPORTANT CLIENT!
RRRING!
AH!... THERE HE IS!
HELLO?... YES... WHO?...
DRAT!
IT'S FOR YOU... IT'S ONE OF THE NEIGHBOURS!...
RRRING!
THIS TIME!...
IT'S YOUR FRIEND PAF!
RRRING!
FINALLY!
HELLO?... I DON'T UNDER-STAND!... SPEAK CLEARLY, PLEASE!...
IT'S... IT'S FOR YOU!!
BWOOF?

Bath Time Tricks

... TO GET THE BONE, HE'LL HAVE TO GET IN THE TUB... THAT'S WHEN WE APPEAR AND GIVE HIM A GOOD BATH!
LOOK OUT!... HERE HE COMES!
HEY! THE CHEWY BONE FELL IN THE WATER!
SPLASH!
NOW WE'LL STAND BACK... AND GET READY TO MOVE!
I CAN'T BELIEVE IT!... THEY ACTUALLY DID IT!
IT'S WORKING! HE'S CONFUSED!
WHAT MADE THEM THINK THAT WOULD BE A GOOD IDEA?
IT'S SO DAFT, I HAVE TO GET IT OUT OF THERE!
SPLOOSH!
!?
?

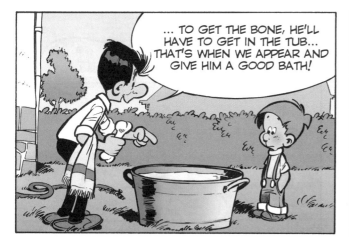

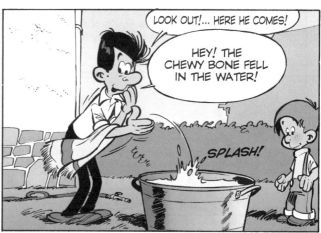

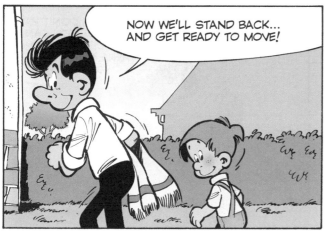

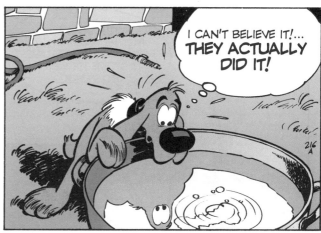

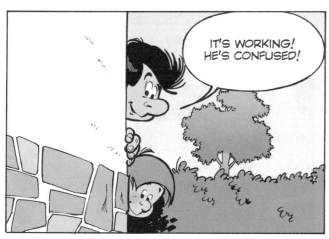

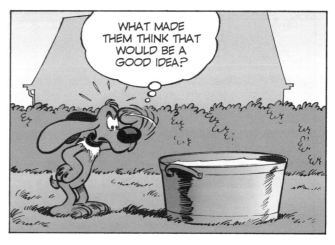

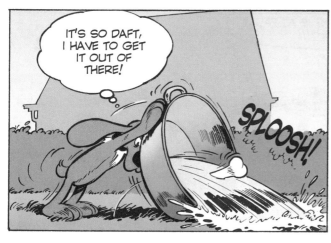

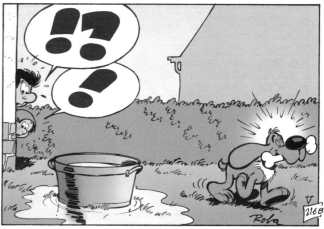

The Great Best Mate

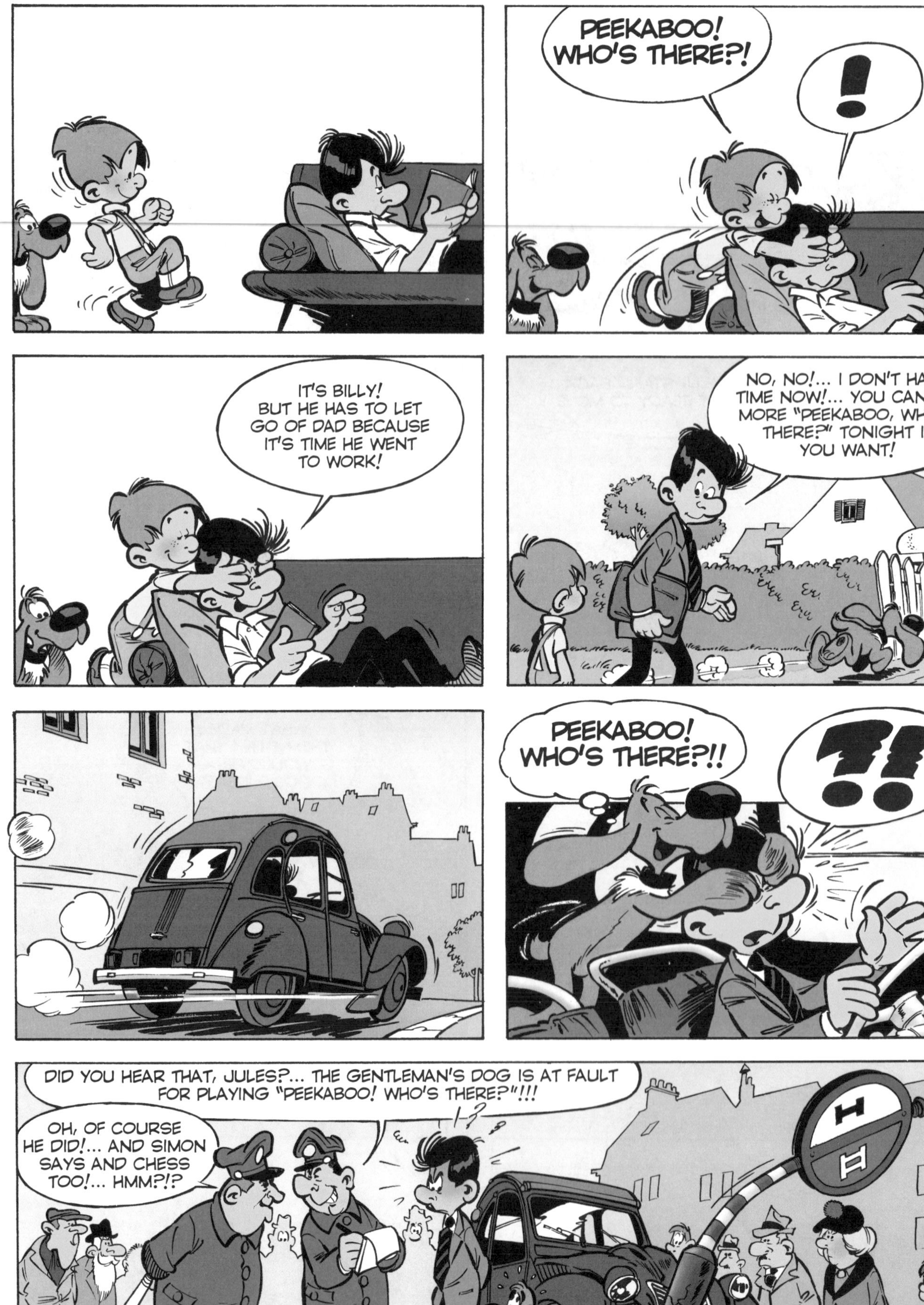
PEEKABOO! WHO'S THERE?!
!
IT'S BILLY! BUT HE HAS TO LET GO OF DAD BECAUSE IT'S TIME HE WENT TO WORK!
NO, NO!... I DON'T HAVE TIME NOW!... YOU CAN DO MORE "PEEKABOO, WHO'S THERE?" TONIGHT IF YOU WANT!
217 A
PEEKABOO! WHO'S THERE?!!
?!
DID YOU HEAR THAT, JULES?... THE GENTLEMAN'S DOG IS AT FAULT FOR PLAYING "PEEKABOO! WHO'S THERE?"!!!
OH, OF COURSE HE DID!... AND SIMON SAYS AND CHESS TOO!... HMM?!?
!-?
H
Roba
217 B

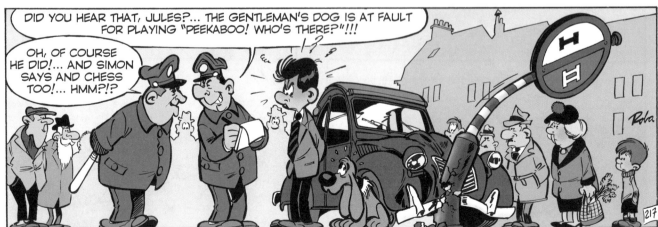

Speech Impediment

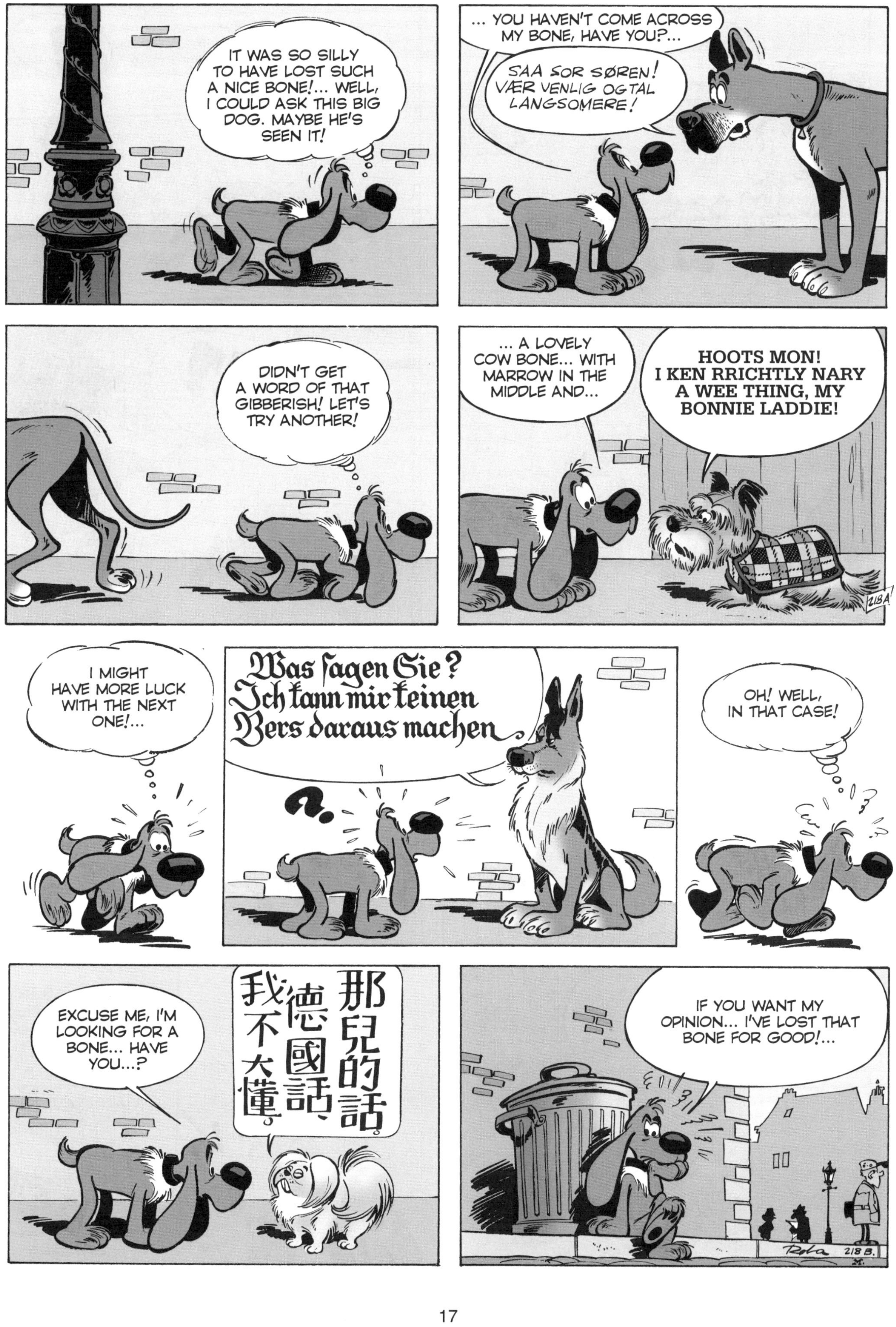
IT WAS SO SILLY TO HAVE LOST SUCH A NICE BONE!... WELL, I COULD ASK THIS BIG DOG. MAYBE HE'S SEEN IT!
... YOU HAVEN'T COME ACROSS MY BONE, HAVE YOU?...
SAA SOR SØREN! VÆR VENLIG OGTAL LANGSOMERE!
DIDN'T GET A WORD OF THAT GIBBERISH! LET'S TRY ANOTHER!
... A LOVELY COW BONE... WITH MARROW IN THE MIDDLE AND...
HOOTS MON! I KEN RRICHTLY NARY A WEE THING, MY BONNIE LADDIE!
I MIGHT HAVE MORE LUCK WITH THE NEXT ONE!...
Was sagen Sie? Ich kann mir keinen Vers daraus machen
OH! WELL, IN THAT CASE!
EXCUSE ME, I'M LOOKING FOR A BONE... HAVE YOU...?
那兒的話。德國話、我不大懂。
IF YOU WANT MY OPINION... I'VE LOST THAT BONE FOR GOOD!...

Doggy Come, Doggy Go

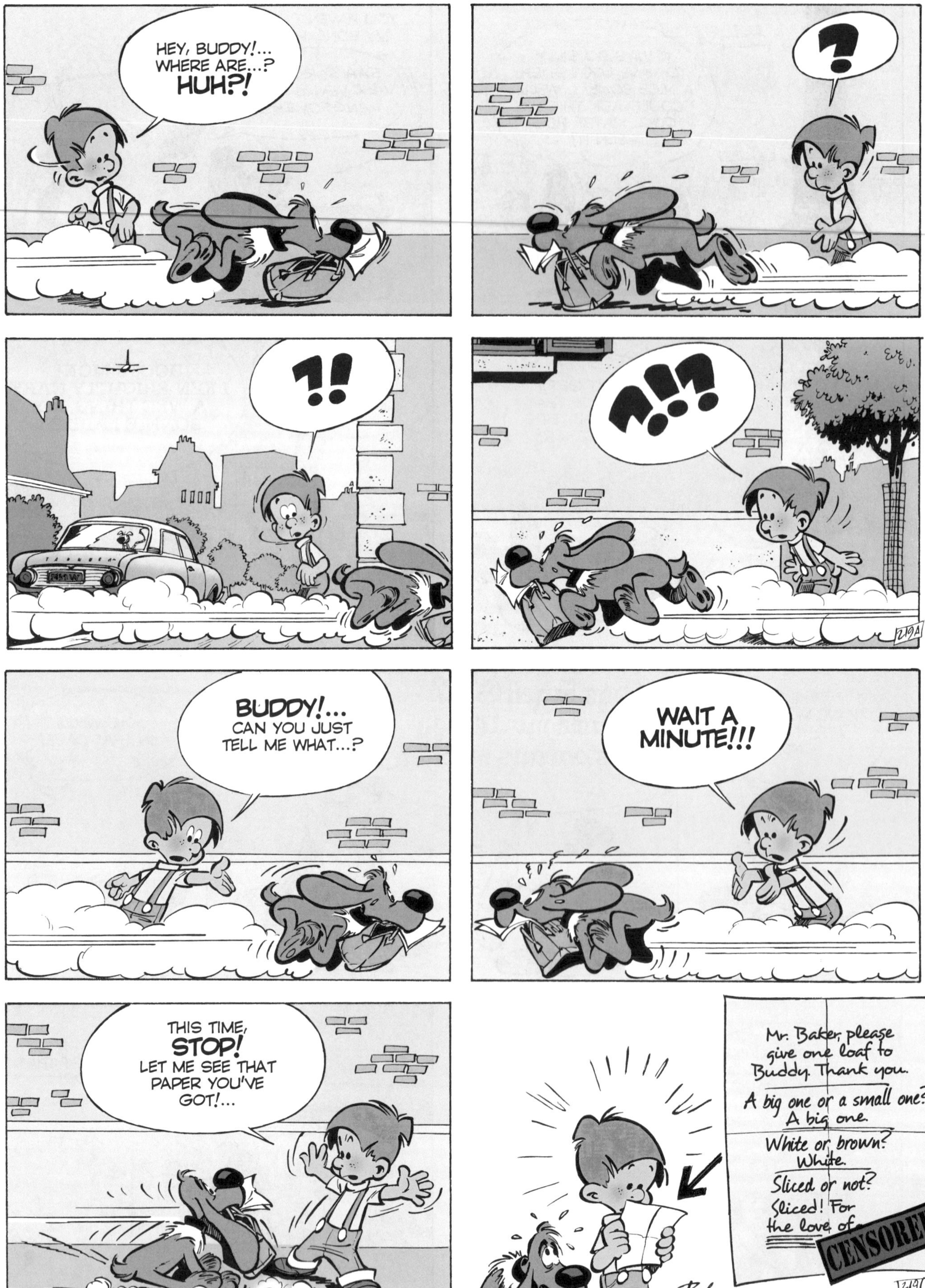
HEY, BUDDY!... WHERE ARE...? HUH?!
?
?!
?!!?
219A
BUDDY!... CAN YOU JUST TELL ME WHAT...?
WAIT A MINUTE!!!
THIS TIME, STOP! LET ME SEE THAT PAPER YOU'VE GOT!...
Mr. Baker, please give one loaf to Buddy. Thank you.
A big one or a small one? A big one.
White or brown? White.
Sliced or not? Sliced! For the love of
CENSORED
Rola
SCRIPT: ISMAËL.
219 B

Soak for a Joke

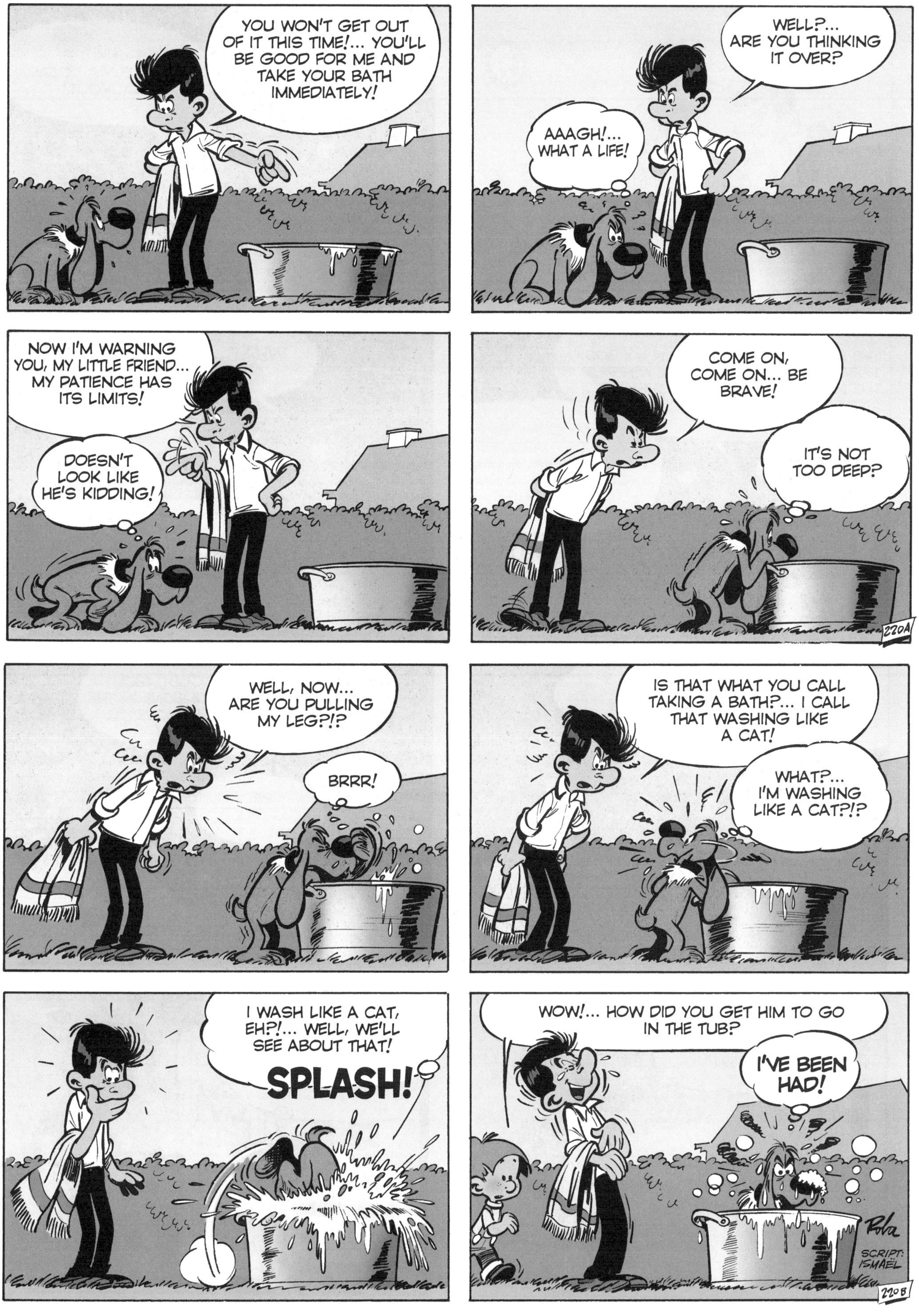
YOU WON'T GET OUT OF IT THIS TIME!... YOU'LL BE GOOD FOR ME AND TAKE YOUR BATH IMMEDIATELY!
WELL?... ARE YOU THINKING IT OVER?
AAAGH!... WHAT A LIFE!
NOW I'M WARNING YOU, MY LITTLE FRIEND... MY PATIENCE HAS ITS LIMITS!
DOESN'T LOOK LIKE HE'S KIDDING!
COME ON, COME ON... BE BRAVE!
IT'S NOT TOO DEEP?
220A
WELL, NOW... ARE YOU PULLING MY LEG?!?
BRRR!
IS THAT WHAT YOU CALL TAKING A BATH?... I CALL THAT WASHING LIKE A CAT!
WHAT?... I'M WASHING LIKE A CAT?!?
I WASH LIKE A CAT, EH?!... WELL, WE'LL SEE ABOUT THAT!
SPLASH!
WOW!... HOW DID YOU GET HIM TO GO IN THE TUB?
I'VE BEEN HAD!
Roba
SCRIPT: ISMAËL
220B

Dark Crimes

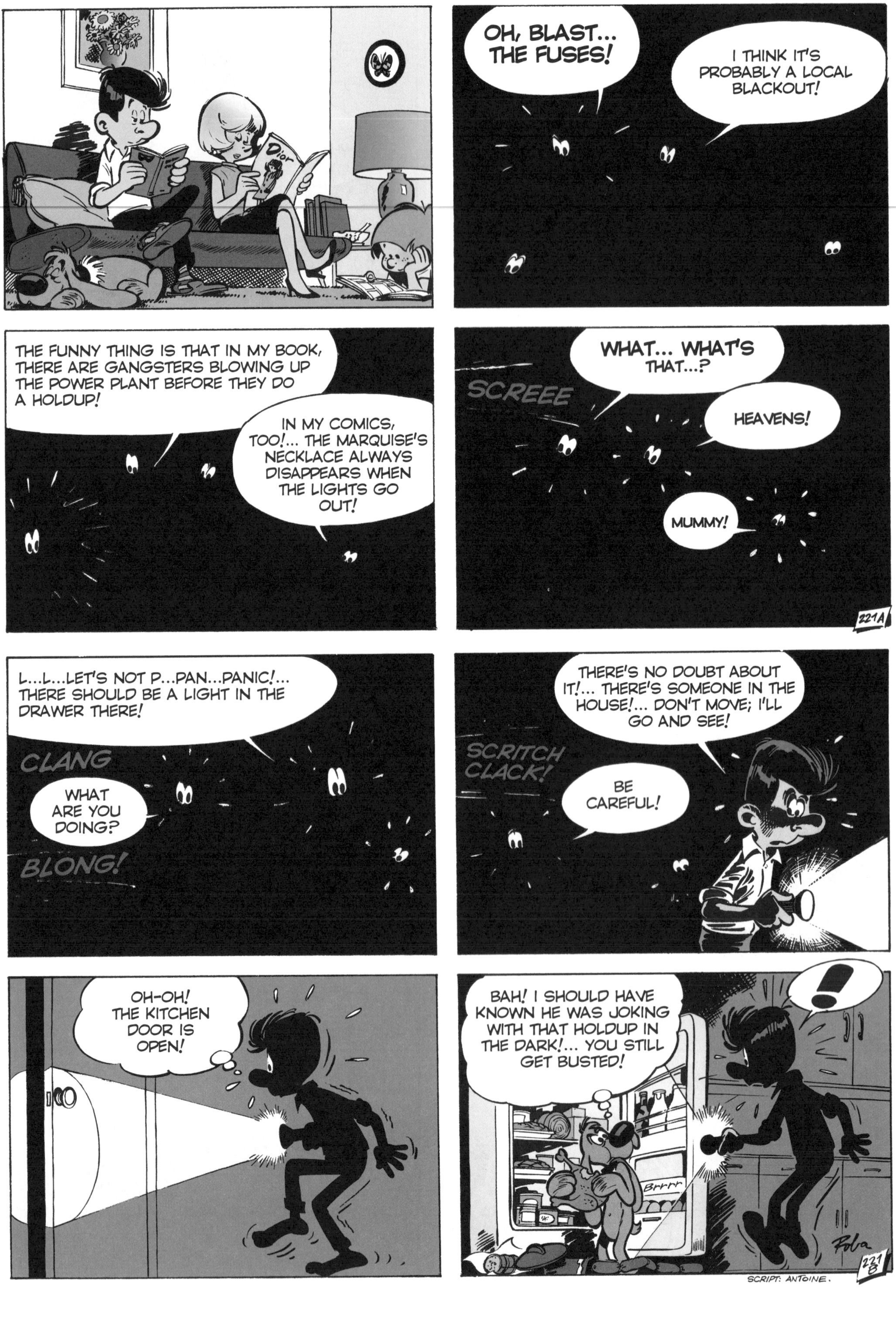

OH, BLAST... THE FUSES!
I THINK IT'S PROBABLY A LOCAL BLACKOUT!
THE FUNNY THING IS THAT IN MY BOOK, THERE ARE GANGSTERS BLOWING UP THE POWER PLANT BEFORE THEY DO A HOLDUP!
IN MY COMICS, TOO!... THE MARQUISE'S NECKLACE ALWAYS DISAPPEARS WHEN THE LIGHTS GO OUT!
SCREEE
WHAT... WHAT'S THAT...?
HEAVENS!
MUMMY!
221A
L...L...LET'S NOT P...PAN...PANIC!... THERE SHOULD BE A LIGHT IN THE DRAWER THERE!
CLANG
WHAT ARE YOU DOING?
BLONG!
THERE'S NO DOUBT ABOUT IT!... THERE'S SOMEONE IN THE HOUSE!... DON'T MOVE; I'LL GO AND SEE!
SCRITCH CLACK!
BE CAREFUL!
OH-OH! THE KITCHEN DOOR IS OPEN!
BAH! I SHOULD HAVE KNOWN HE WAS JOKING WITH THAT HOLDUP IN THE DARK!... YOU STILL GET BUSTED!
!
Brrrr
221 B
SCRIPT: ANTOINE.

Hoarse-play

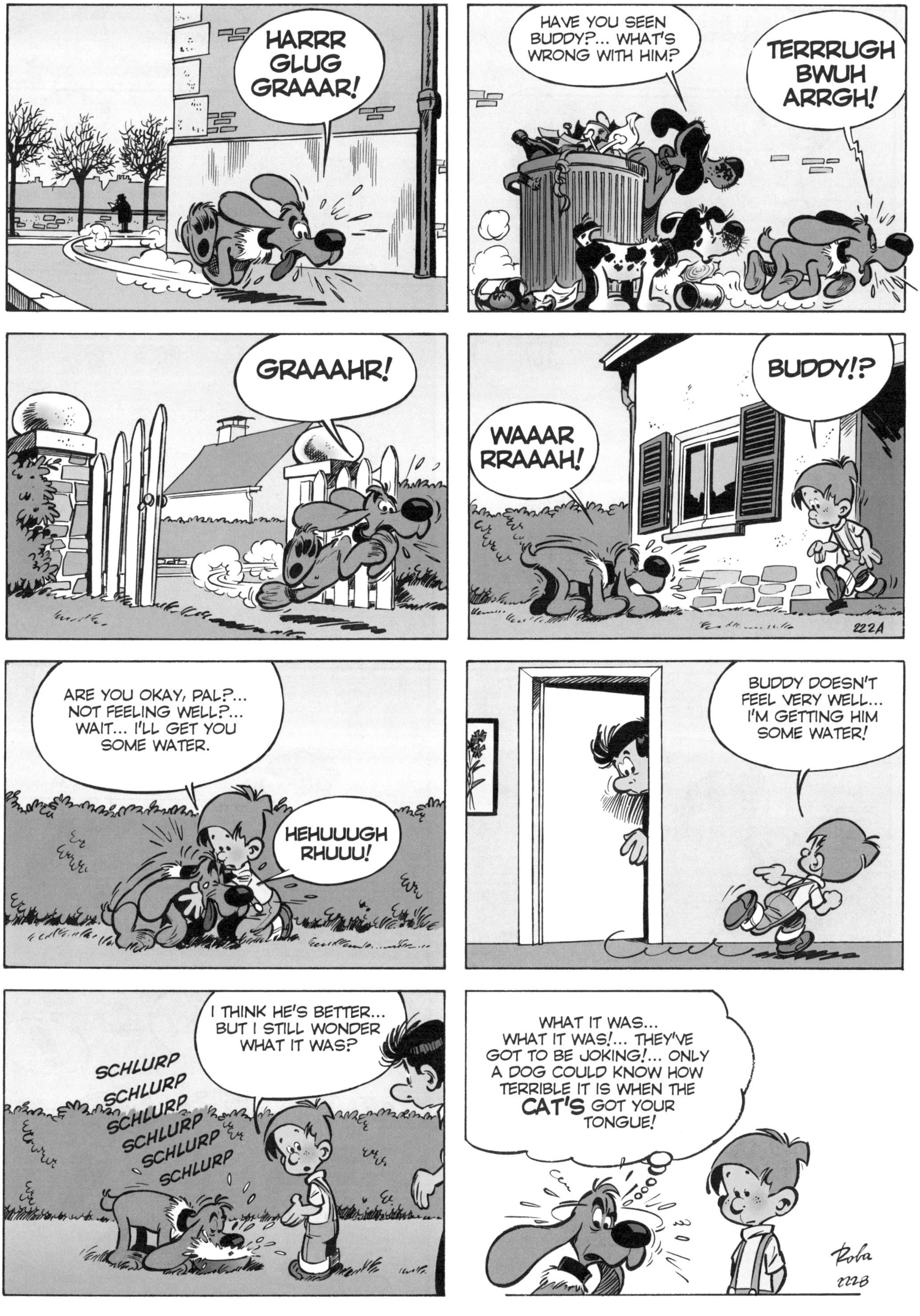
HARRR GLUG GRAAAR!
HAVE YOU SEEN BUDDY?... WHAT'S WRONG WITH HIM?
TERRRUGH BWUH ARRGH!
GRAAAHR!
WAAAR RRAAAH!
BUDDY!?
222A
ARE YOU OKAY, PAL?... NOT FEELING WELL?... WAIT... I'LL GET YOU SOME WATER.
HEHUUUGH RHUUU!
BUDDY DOESN'T FEEL VERY WELL... I'M GETTING HIM SOME WATER!
I THINK HE'S BETTER... BUT I STILL WONDER WHAT IT WAS?
SCHLURP
SCHLURP
SCHLURP
SCHLURP
SCHLURP
SCHLURP
WHAT IT WAS... WHAT IT WAS!... THEY'VE GOT TO BE JOKING!... ONLY A DOG COULD KNOW HOW TERRIBLE IT IS WHEN THE CAT'S GOT YOUR TONGUE!
Roba
222B

Yoyomania

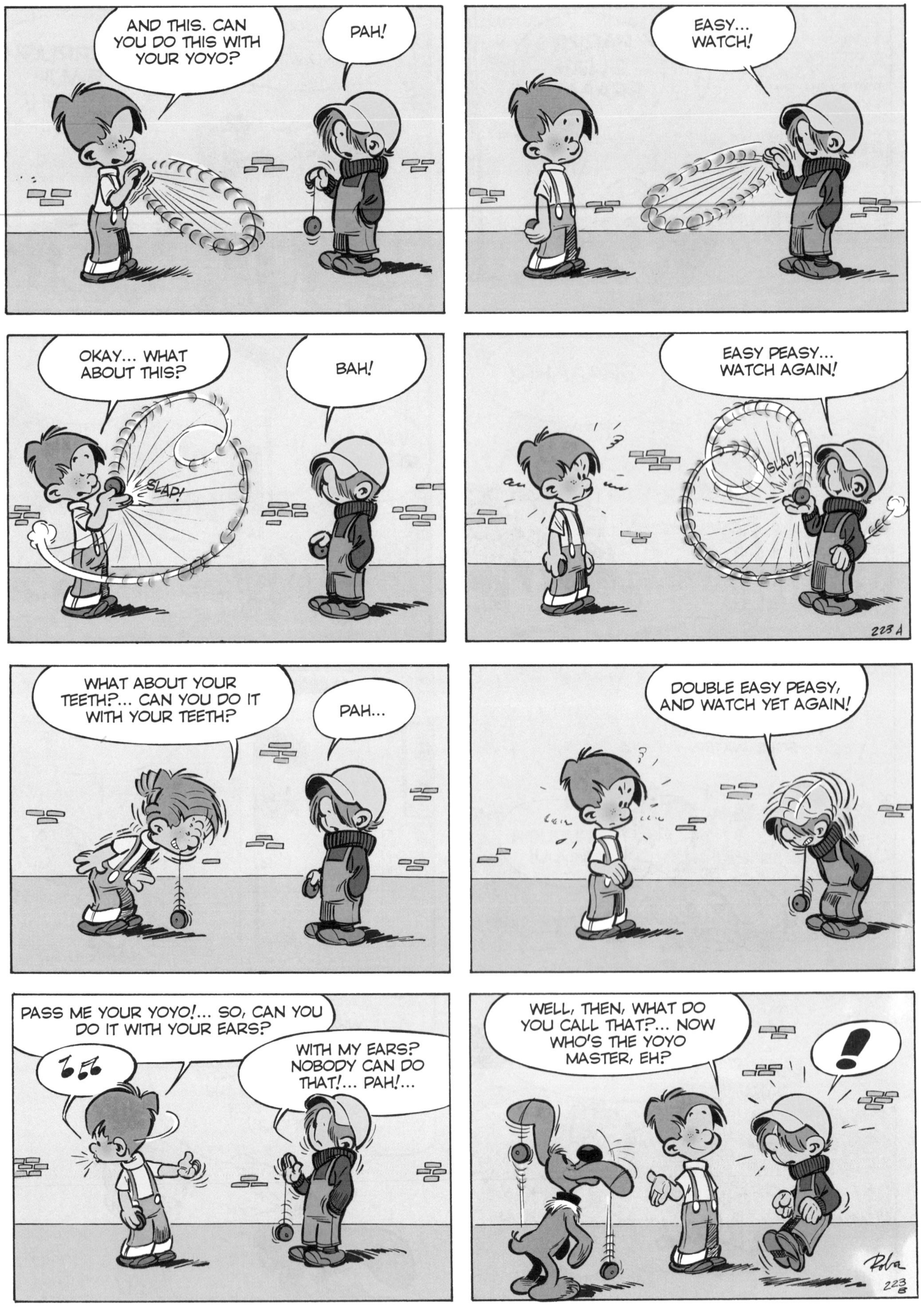

AND THIS. CAN YOU DO THIS WITH YOUR YOYO?
PAH!
EASY... WATCH!
OKAY... WHAT ABOUT THIS?
SLAP!
BAH!
EASY PEASY... WATCH AGAIN!
SLAP!
223 A
WHAT ABOUT YOUR TEETH?... CAN YOU DO IT WITH YOUR TEETH?
PAH...
DOUBLE EASY PEASY, AND WATCH YET AGAIN!
PASS ME YOUR YOYO!... SO, CAN YOU DO IT WITH YOUR EARS?
WITH MY EARS? NOBODY CAN DO THAT!... PAH!...
WELL, THEN, WHAT DO YOU CALL THAT?... NOW WHO'S THE YOYO MASTER, EH?
!
Roba
223 B

Charity Begins at Bone

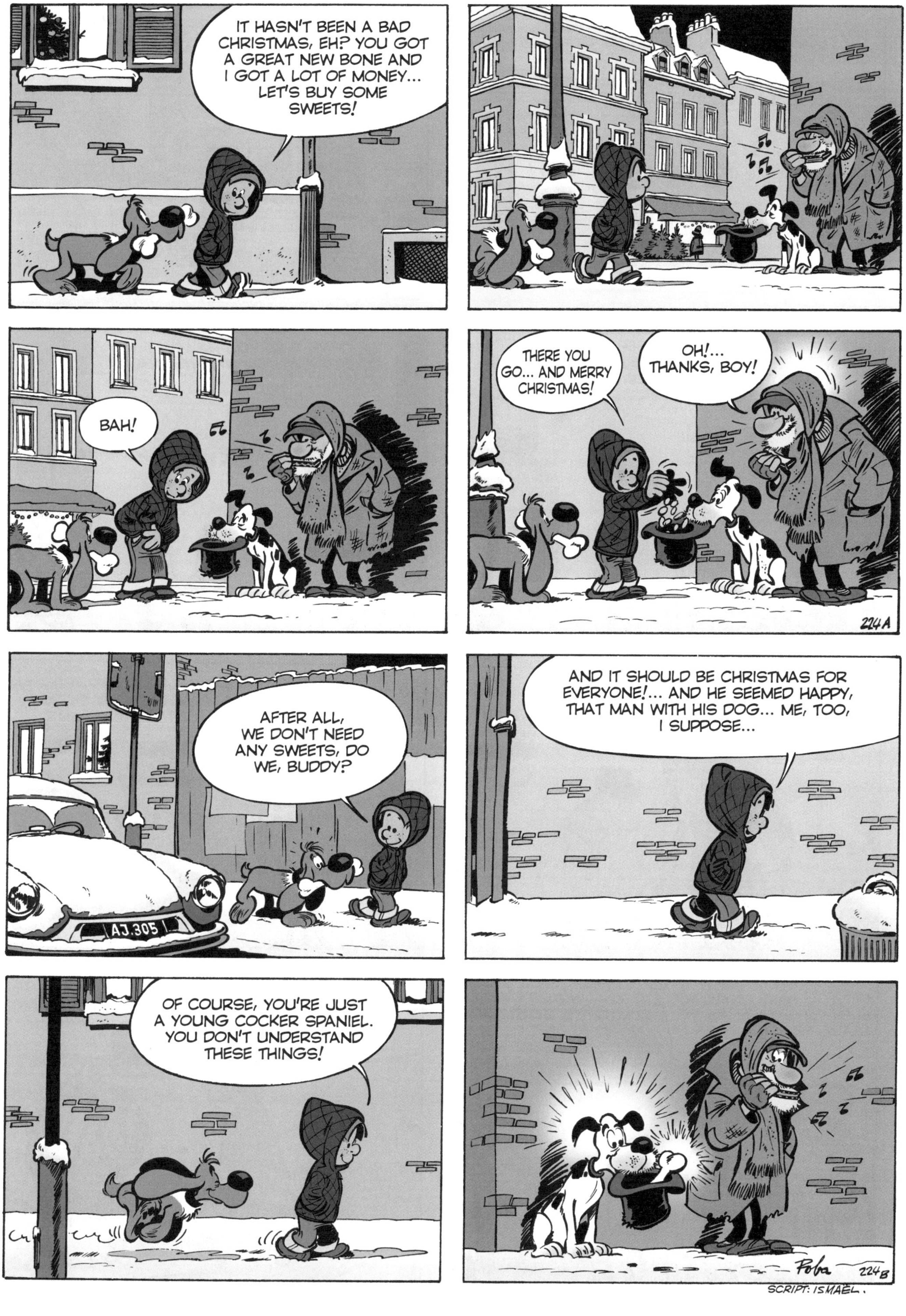
IT HASN'T BEEN A BAD CHRISTMAS, EH? YOU GOT A GREAT NEW BONE AND I GOT A LOT OF MONEY... LET'S BUY SOME SWEETS!
BAH!
THERE YOU GO... AND MERRY CHRISTMAS!
OH!... THANKS, BOY!
224 A
AFTER ALL, WE DON'T NEED ANY SWEETS, DO WE, BUDDY?
AJ.305
AND IT SHOULD BE CHRISTMAS FOR EVERYONE!... AND HE SEEMED HAPPY, THAT MAN WITH HIS DOG... ME, TOO, I SUPPOSE...
OF COURSE, YOU'RE JUST A YOUNG COCKER SPANIEL. YOU DON'T UNDERSTAND THESE THINGS!
Roba 224B

SCRIPT: ISMAEL.

Protection Selection

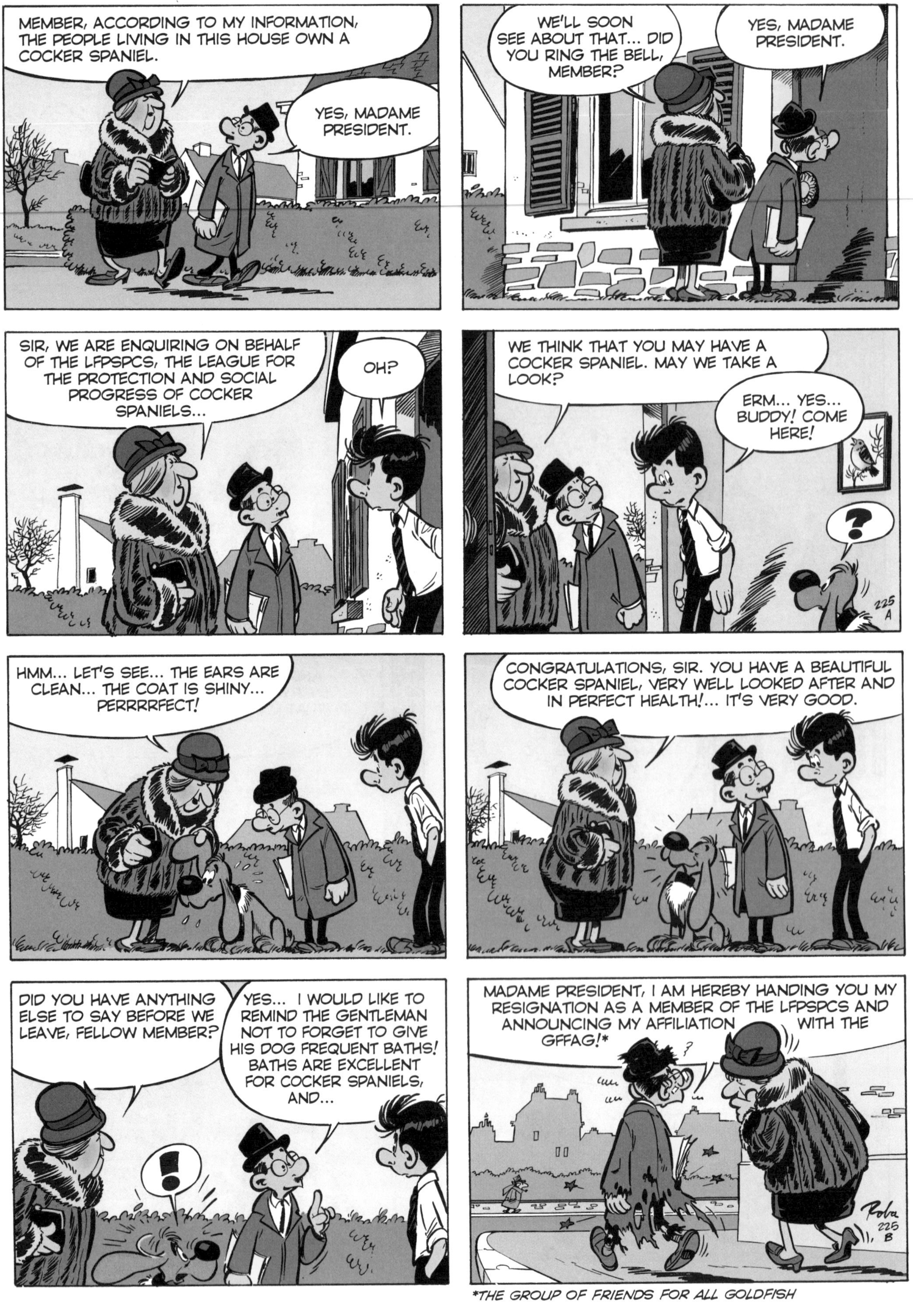
MEMBER, ACCORDING TO MY INFORMATION, THE PEOPLE LIVING IN THIS HOUSE OWN A COCKER SPANIEL.
YES, MADAME PRESIDENT.
WE'LL SOON SEE ABOUT THAT... DID YOU RING THE BELL, MEMBER?
YES, MADAME PRESIDENT.
SIR, WE ARE ENQUIRING ON BEHALF OF THE LFPSPCS, THE LEAGUE FOR THE PROTECTION AND SOCIAL PROGRESS OF COCKER SPANIELS...
OH?
WE THINK THAT YOU MAY HAVE A COCKER SPANIEL. MAY WE TAKE A LOOK?
ERM... YES... BUDDY! COME HERE!
?
HMM... LET'S SEE... THE EARS ARE CLEAN... THE COAT IS SHINY... PERRRRFECT!
CONGRATULATIONS, SIR. YOU HAVE A BEAUTIFUL COCKER SPANIEL, VERY WELL LOOKED AFTER AND IN PERFECT HEALTH!... IT'S VERY GOOD.
DID YOU HAVE ANYTHING ELSE TO SAY BEFORE WE LEAVE, FELLOW MEMBER?
YES... I WOULD LIKE TO REMIND THE GENTLEMAN NOT TO FORGET TO GIVE HIS DOG FREQUENT BATHS! BATHS ARE EXCELLENT FOR COCKER SPANIELS, AND...
!
MADAME PRESIDENT, I AM HEREBY HANDING YOU MY RESIGNATION AS A MEMBER OF THE LFPSPCS AND ANNOUNCING MY AFFILIATION WITH THE GFFAG!*
Roba

**THE GROUP OF FRIENDS FOR ALL GOLDFISH*

Ooh, yeah, New Year!

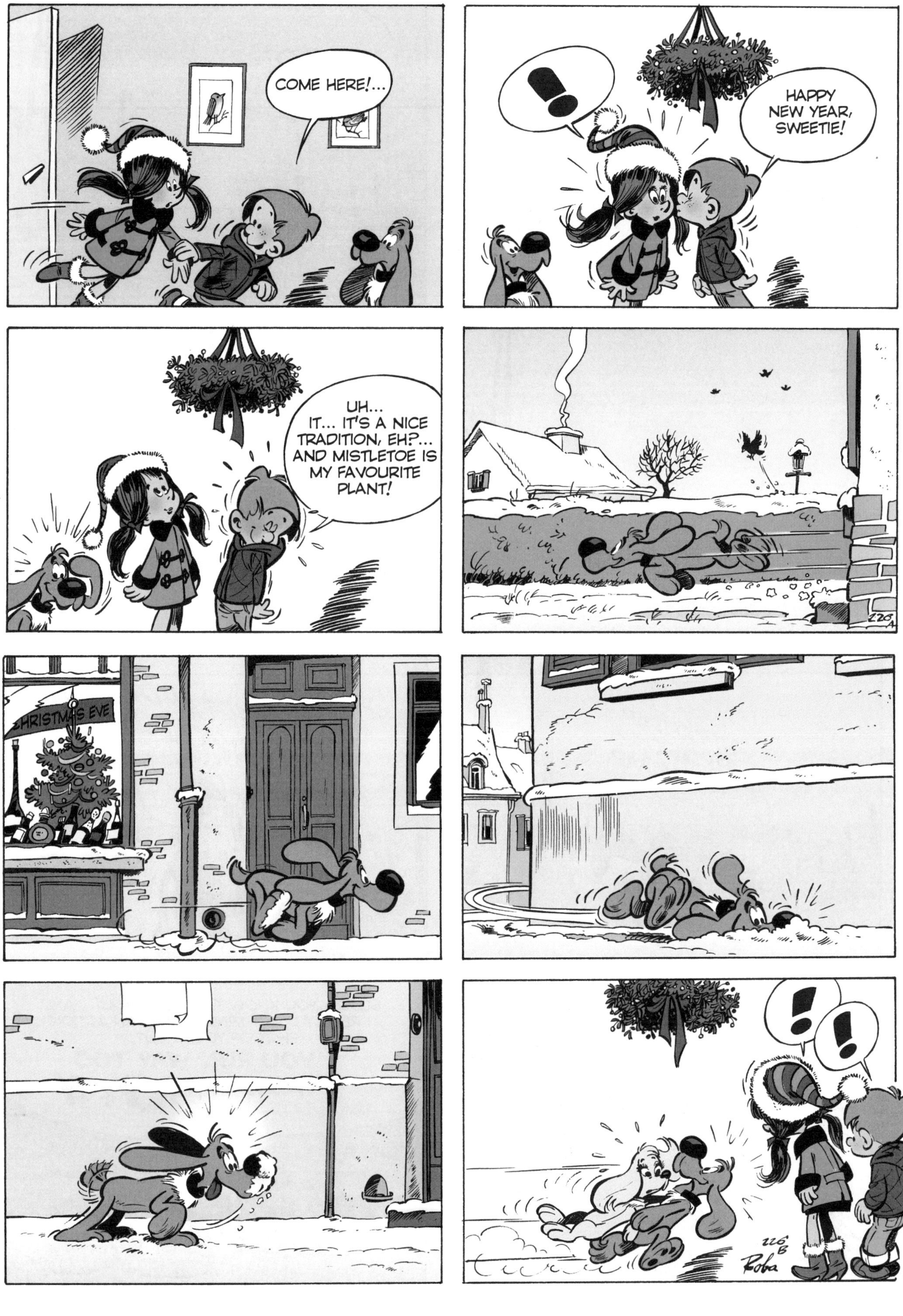
COME HERE!...
HAPPY NEW YEAR, SWEETIE!
UH... IT... IT'S A NICE TRADITION, EH?... AND MISTLETOE IS MY FAVOURITE PLANT!
CHRISTMAS EVE
Roba

And action!

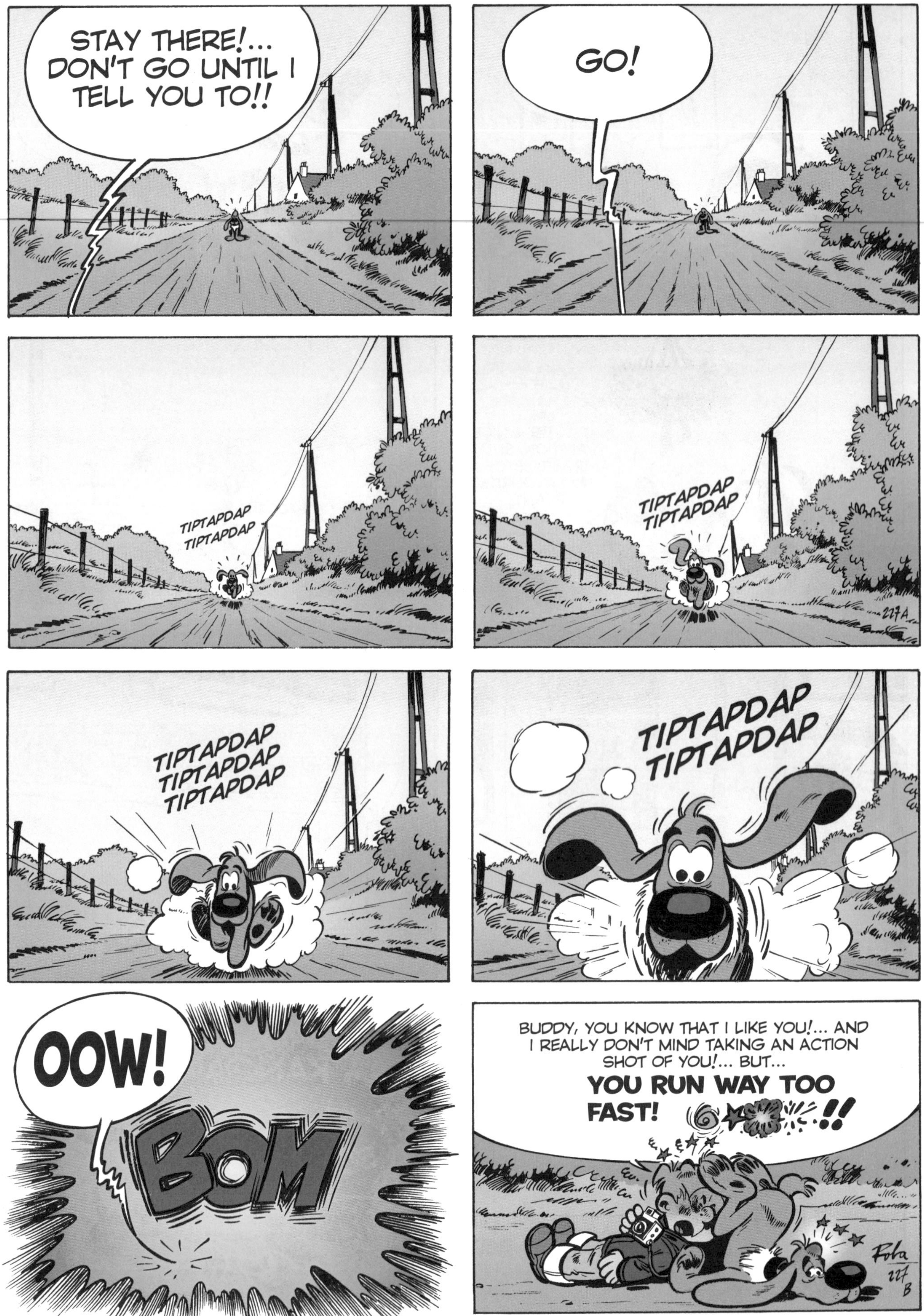
STAY THERE!... DON'T GO UNTIL I TELL YOU TO!!
GO!
TIPTAPDAP TIPTAPDAP
TIPTAPDAP TIPTAPDAP
TIPTAPDAP TIPTAPDAP TIPTAPDAP
TIPTAPDAP TIPTAPDAP
OOW!
BOM
BUDDY, YOU KNOW THAT I LIKE YOU!... AND I REALLY DON'T MIND TAKING AN ACTION SHOT OF YOU!... BUT...
YOU RUN WAY TOO FAST!

Apocketlypse

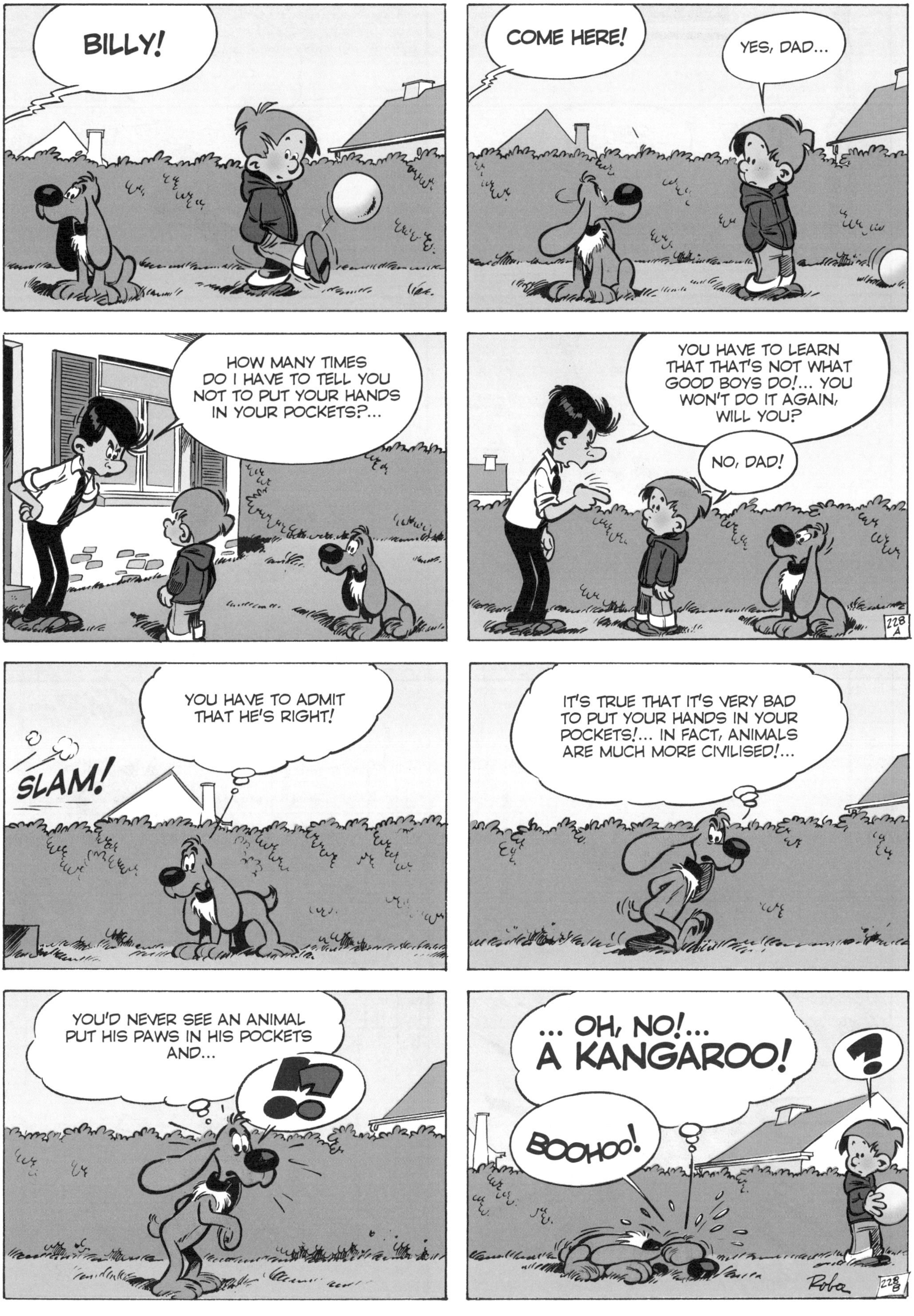

BILLY!
COME HERE!
YES, DAD...
HOW MANY TIMES DO I HAVE TO TELL YOU NOT TO PUT YOUR HANDS IN YOUR POCKETS?...
YOU HAVE TO LEARN THAT THAT'S NOT WHAT GOOD BOYS DO!... YOU WON'T DO IT AGAIN, WILL YOU?
NO, DAD!
228 A
SLAM!
YOU HAVE TO ADMIT THAT HE'S RIGHT!
IT'S TRUE THAT IT'S VERY BAD TO PUT YOUR HANDS IN YOUR POCKETS!... IN FACT, ANIMALS ARE MUCH MORE CIVILISED!...
YOU'D NEVER SEE AN ANIMAL PUT HIS PAWS IN HIS POCKETS AND...
... OH, NO!... A KANGAROO!
?
BOOHOO!
Roba
228 B

The Bone Collector

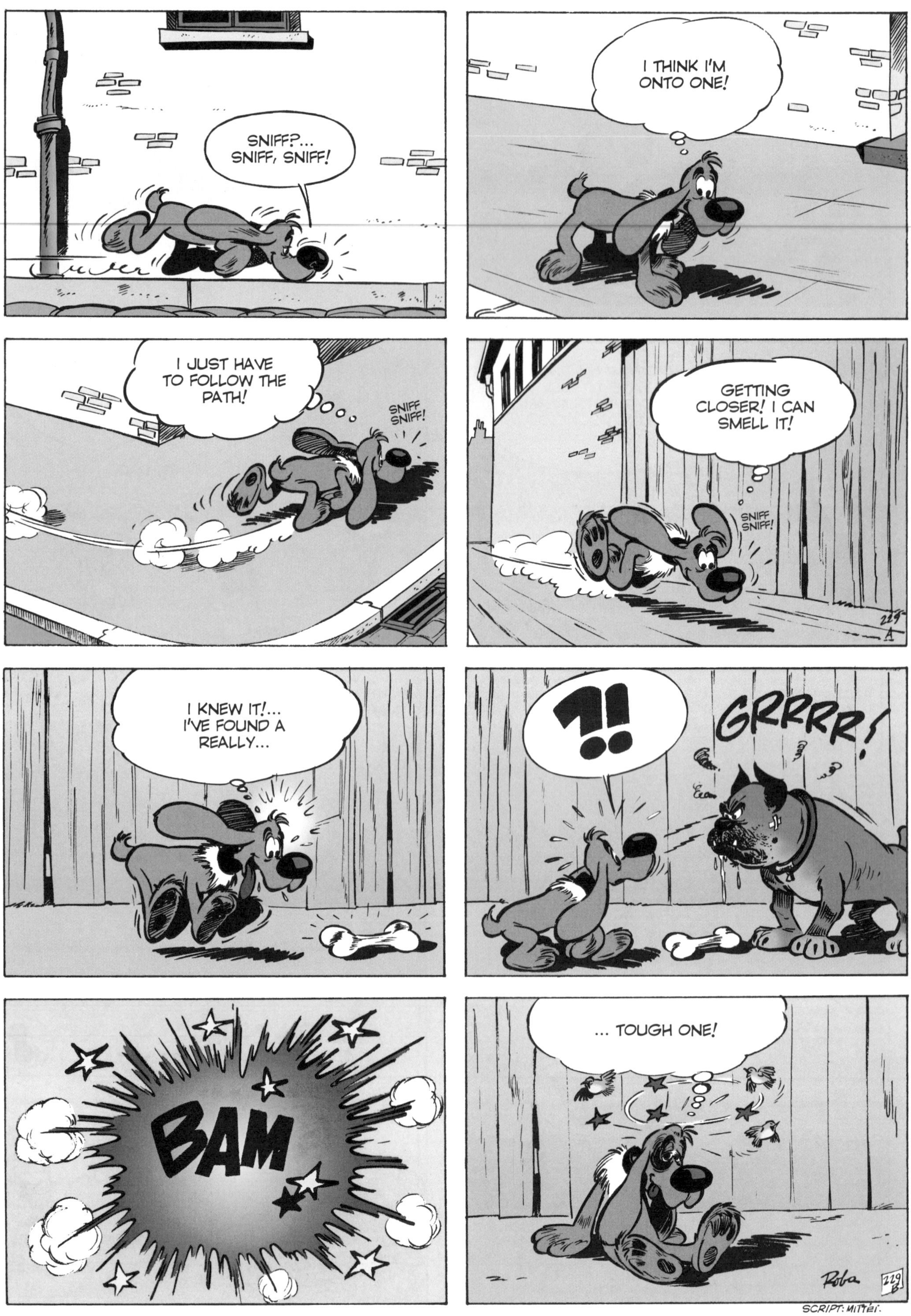
SNIFF?... SNIFF, SNIFF!
I THINK I'M ONTO ONE!
I JUST HAVE TO FOLLOW THE PATH!
SNIFF SNIFF!
GETTING CLOSER! I CAN SMELL IT!
SNIFF SNIFF!
I KNEW IT!... I'VE FOUND A REALLY...
?!
GRRRR!
BAM
... TOUGH ONE!
Roba

SCRIPT: MITTEI.

A Load of Road Code

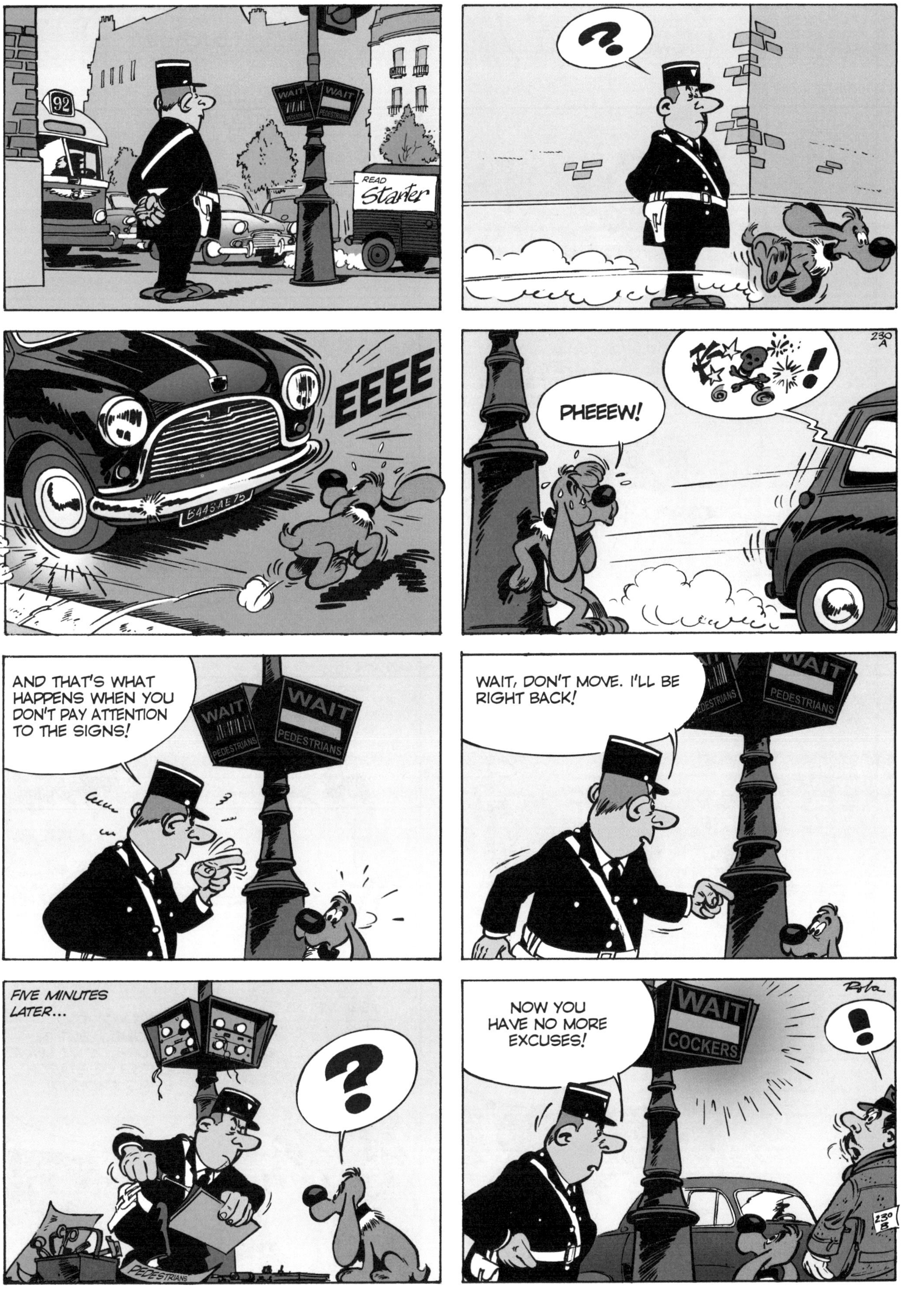
92
WAIT
PEDESTRIANS
READ Starter
?
EEEE
230 A
PHEEEW!
!
AND THAT'S WHAT HAPPENS WHEN YOU DON'T PAY ATTENTION TO THE SIGNS!
WAIT
PEDESTRIANS
WAIT, DON'T MOVE. I'LL BE RIGHT BACK!
FIVE MINUTES LATER...
?
PEDESTRIANS
NOW YOU HAVE NO MORE EXCUSES!
WAIT
COCKERS
!
Roba
230 B

Stiff Upper Hip

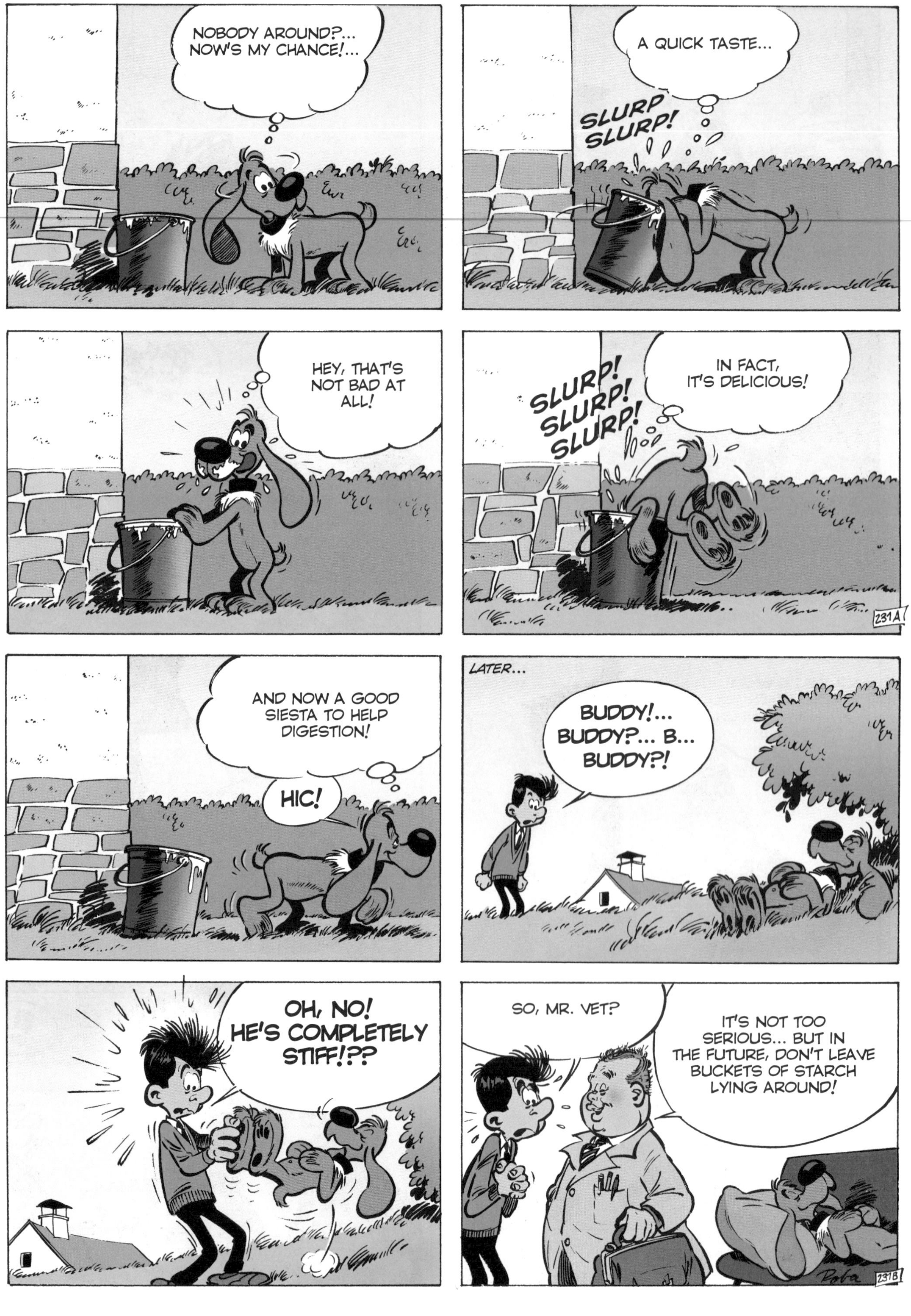
NOBODY AROUND?... NOW'S MY CHANCE!...
A QUICK TASTE...
SLURP SLURP!
HEY, THAT'S NOT BAD AT ALL!
SLURP! SLURP! SLURP!
IN FACT, IT'S DELICIOUS!
231 A
AND NOW A GOOD SIESTA TO HELP DIGESTION!
HIC!
LATER...
BUDDY!... BUDDY?... B... BUDDY?!
OH, NO! HE'S COMPLETELY STIFF!??
SO, MR. VET?
IT'S NOT TOO SERIOUS... BUT IN THE FUTURE, DON'T LEAVE BUCKETS OF STARCH LYING AROUND!
Roba
231 B

Sometimes You Have to Give In

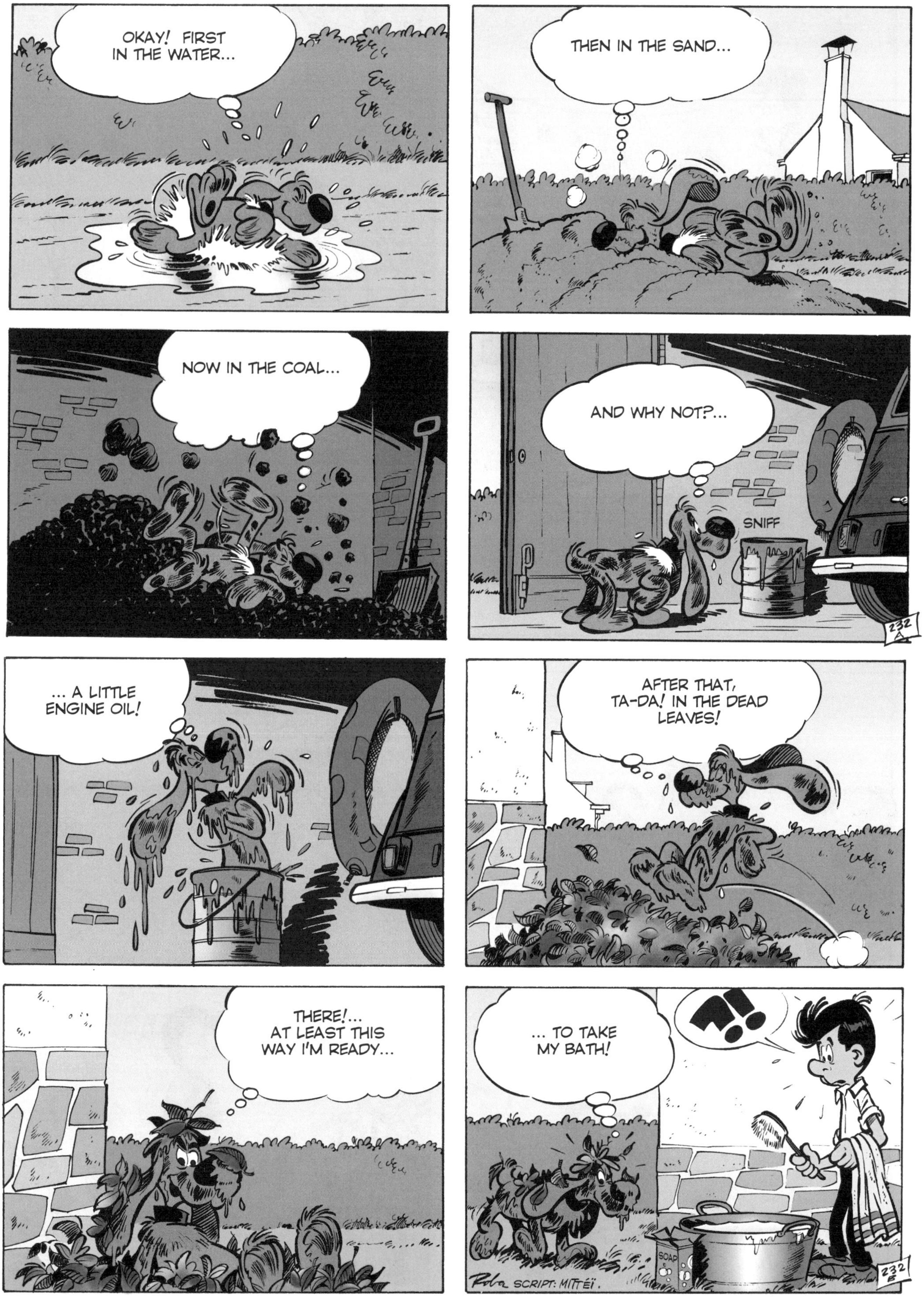

OKAY! FIRST IN THE WATER...
THEN IN THE SAND...
NOW IN THE COAL...
AND WHY NOT?...
SNIFF
... A LITTLE ENGINE OIL!
AFTER THAT, TA-DA! IN THE DEAD LEAVES!
THERE!... AT LEAST THIS WAY I'M READY...
... TO TAKE MY BATH!
SOAP
SCRIPT: MITTÉÏ

Dogtelligence

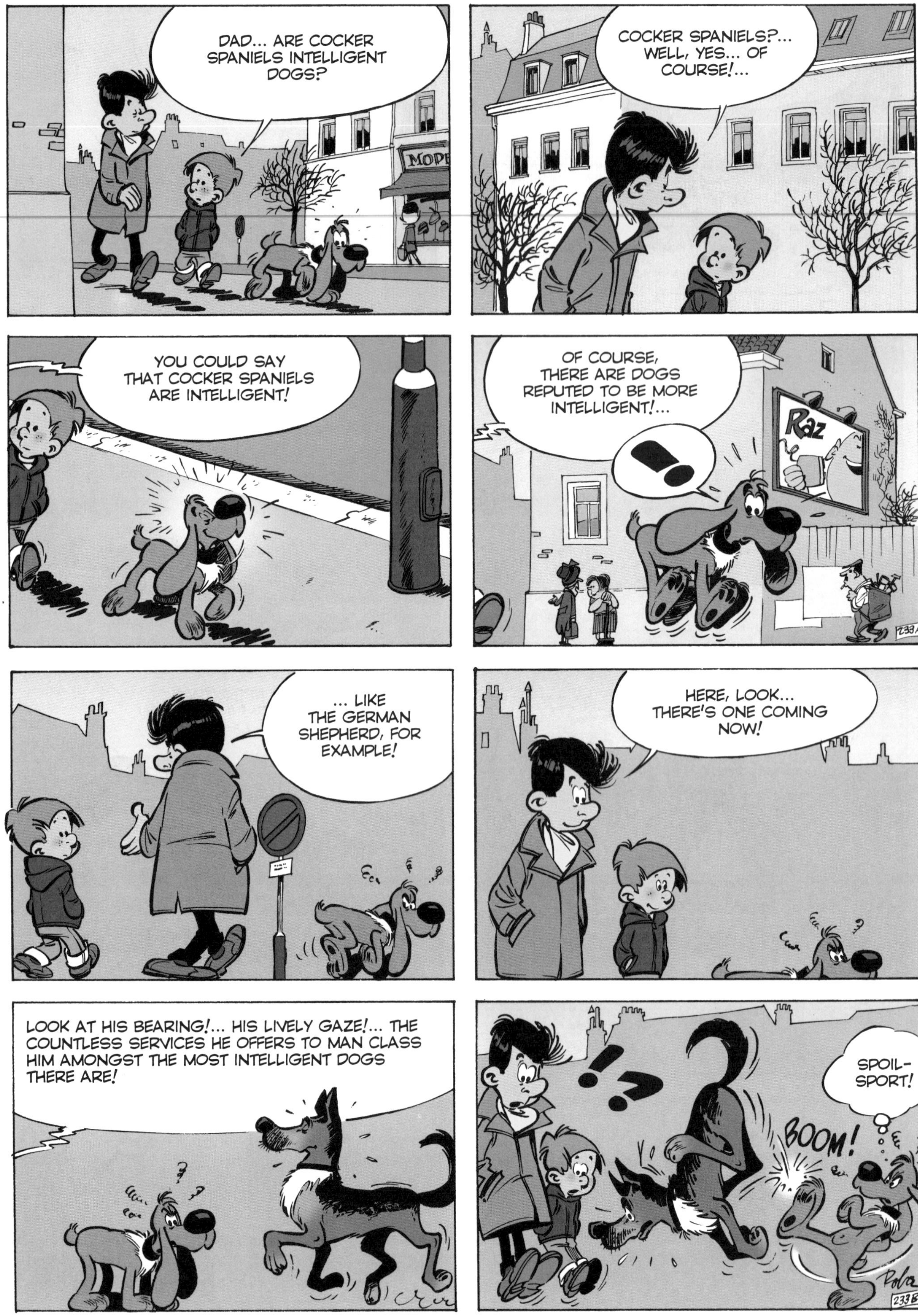

DAD... ARE COCKER SPANIELS INTELLIGENT DOGS?
MOPE
COCKER SPANIELS?... WELL, YES... OF COURSE!...
YOU COULD SAY THAT COCKER SPANIELS ARE INTELLIGENT!
OF COURSE, THERE ARE DOGS REPUTED TO BE MORE INTELLIGENT!...
Raz
233A
... LIKE THE GERMAN SHEPHERD, FOR EXAMPLE!
HERE, LOOK... THERE'S ONE COMING NOW!
LOOK AT HIS BEARING!... HIS LIVELY GAZE!... THE COUNTLESS SERVICES HE OFFERS TO MAN CLASS HIM AMONGST THE MOST INTELLIGENT DOGS THERE ARE!
!?
BOOM!
SPOIL-SPORT!
Roba
233B

Model Dog

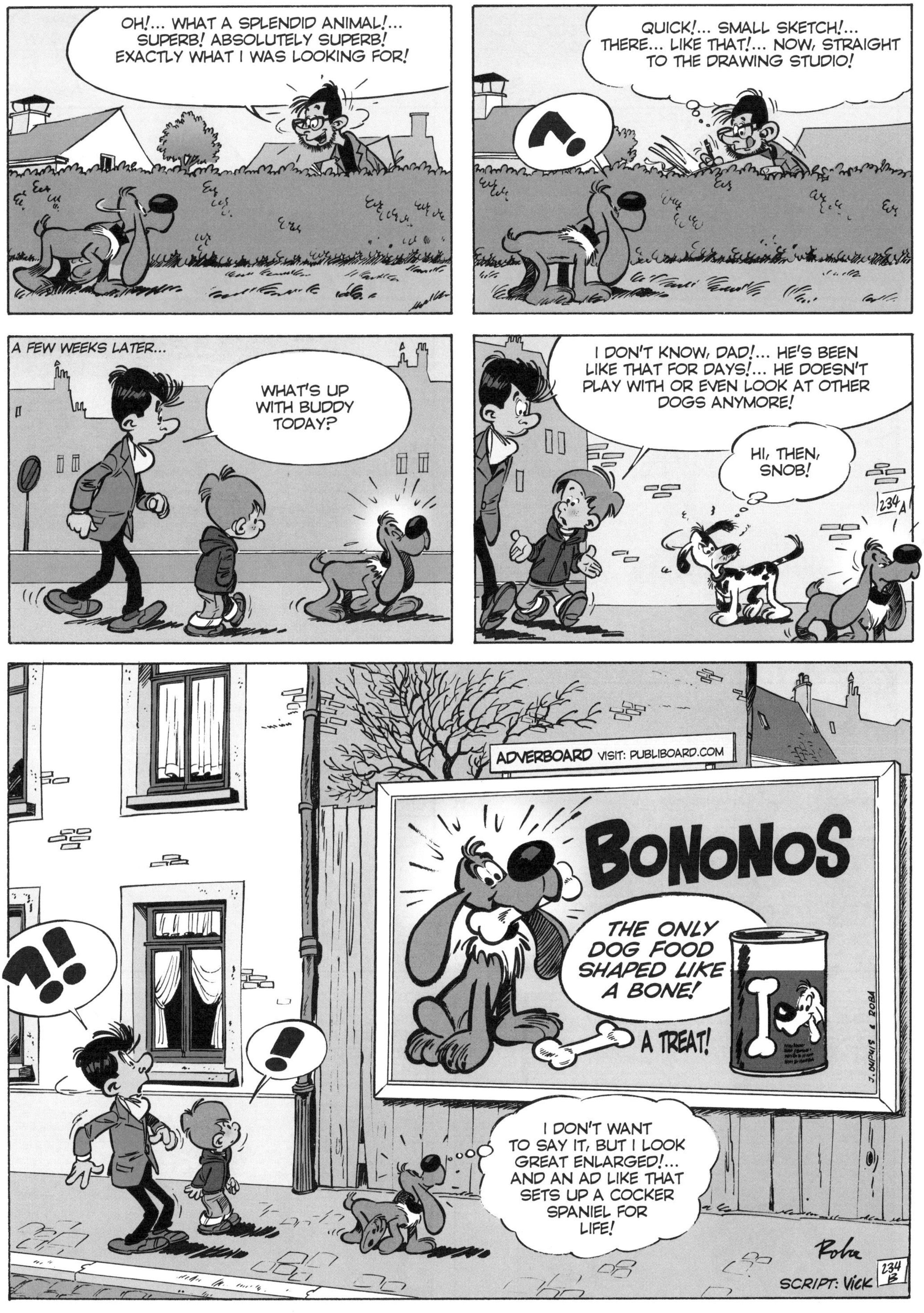
OH!... WHAT A SPLENDID ANIMAL!... SUPERB! ABSOLUTELY SUPERB! EXACTLY WHAT I WAS LOOKING FOR!
QUICK!... SMALL SKETCH!... THERE... LIKE THAT!... NOW, STRAIGHT TO THE DRAWING STUDIO!
?!
A FEW WEEKS LATER...
WHAT'S UP WITH BUDDY TODAY?
I DON'T KNOW, DAD!... HE'S BEEN LIKE THAT FOR DAYS!... HE DOESN'T PLAY WITH OR EVEN LOOK AT OTHER DOGS ANYMORE!
HI, THEN, SNOB!
234 A
ADVERBOARD VISIT: PUBLIBOARD.COM
BONONOS
THE ONLY DOG FOOD SHAPED LIKE A BONE!
A TREAT!
J. DUPUIS & ROBA
?!
!
I DON'T WANT TO SAY IT, BUT I LOOK GREAT ENLARGED!... AND AN AD LIKE THAT SETS UP A COCKER SPANIEL FOR LIFE!
Roba
234 B
SCRIPT: VICK

Lost and Found

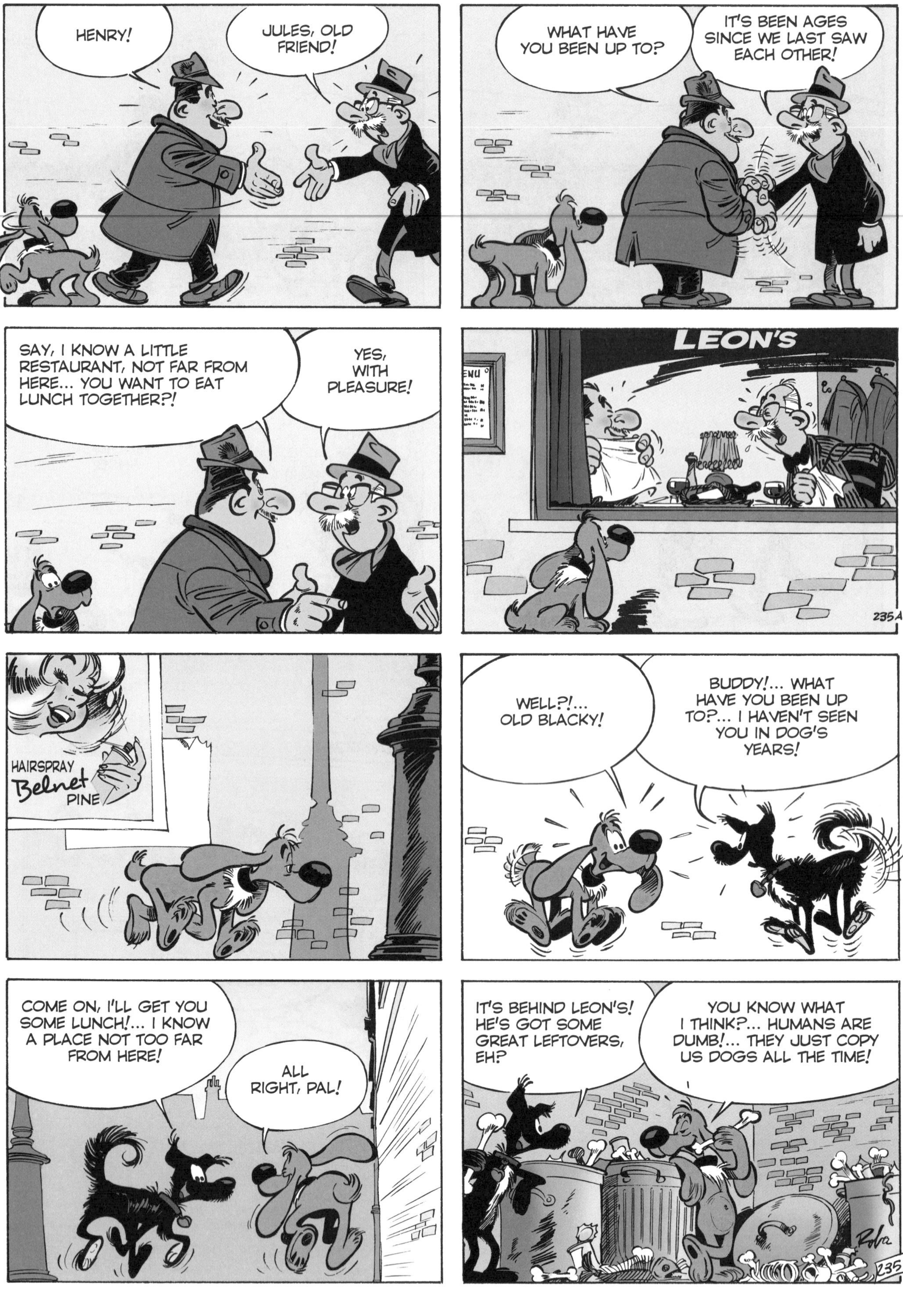
HENRY!
JULES, OLD FRIEND!
WHAT HAVE YOU BEEN UP TO?
IT'S BEEN AGES SINCE WE LAST SAW EACH OTHER!
SAY, I KNOW A LITTLE RESTAURANT, NOT FAR FROM HERE... YOU WANT TO EAT LUNCH TOGETHER?!
YES, WITH PLEASURE!
LEON'S
235A
HAIRSPRAY Belnet PINE
WELL?!... OLD BLACKY!
BUDDY!... WHAT HAVE YOU BEEN UP TO?... I HAVEN'T SEEN YOU IN DOG'S YEARS!
COME ON, I'LL GET YOU SOME LUNCH!... I KNOW A PLACE NOT TOO FAR FROM HERE!
ALL RIGHT, PAL!
IT'S BEHIND LEON'S! HE'S GOT SOME GREAT LEFTOVERS, EH?
YOU KNOW WHAT I THINK?... HUMANS ARE DUMB!... THEY JUST COPY US DOGS ALL THE TIME!
Roba
235B

Take the Ball by the Horns

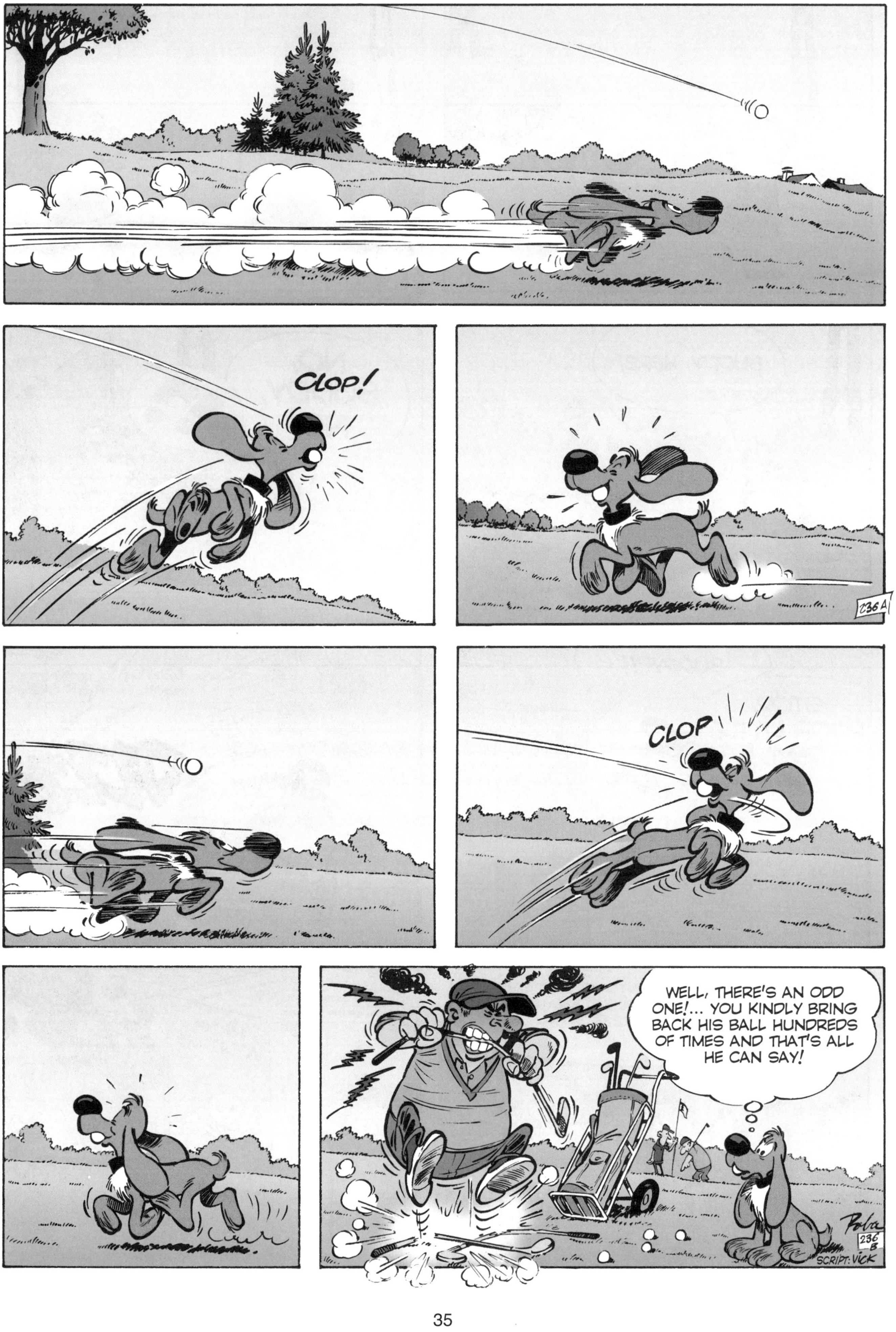
CLOP!
236 A
CLOP
WELL, THERE'S AN ODD ONE!... YOU KINDLY BRING BACK HIS BALL HUNDREDS OF TIMES AND THAT'S ALL HE CAN SAY!
236 B
SCRIPT: VICK

Bad Sign

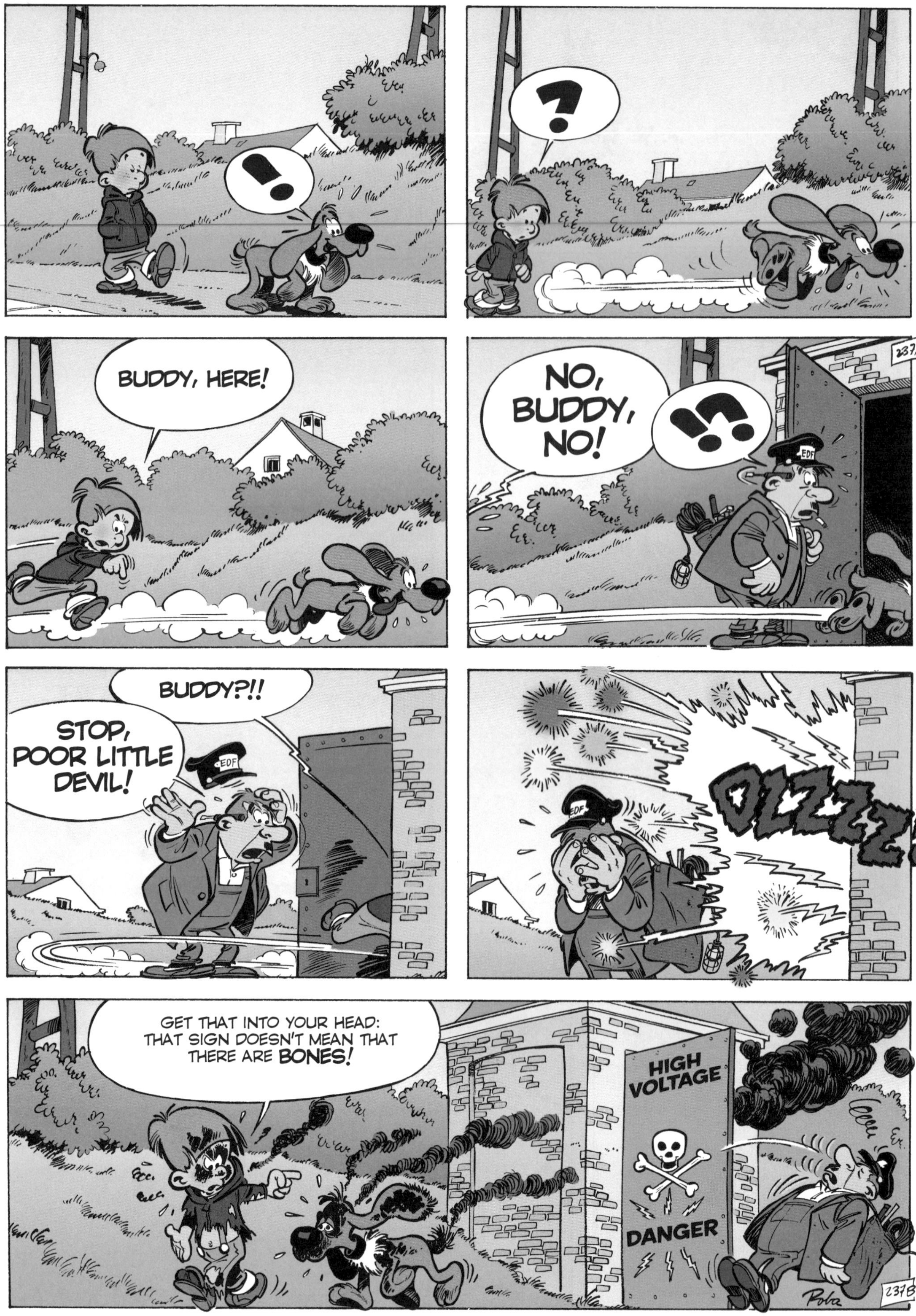

BUDDY, HERE!
237A
NO, BUDDY, NO!
EDF
BUDDY?!!
STOP, POOR LITTLE DEVIL!
EDF
EDF
DZZZZ!
GET THAT INTO YOUR HEAD: THAT SIGN DOESN'T MEAN THAT THERE ARE **BONES**!
HIGH VOLTAGE
DANGER
Roba
237B

No Gain without Pain When You Train

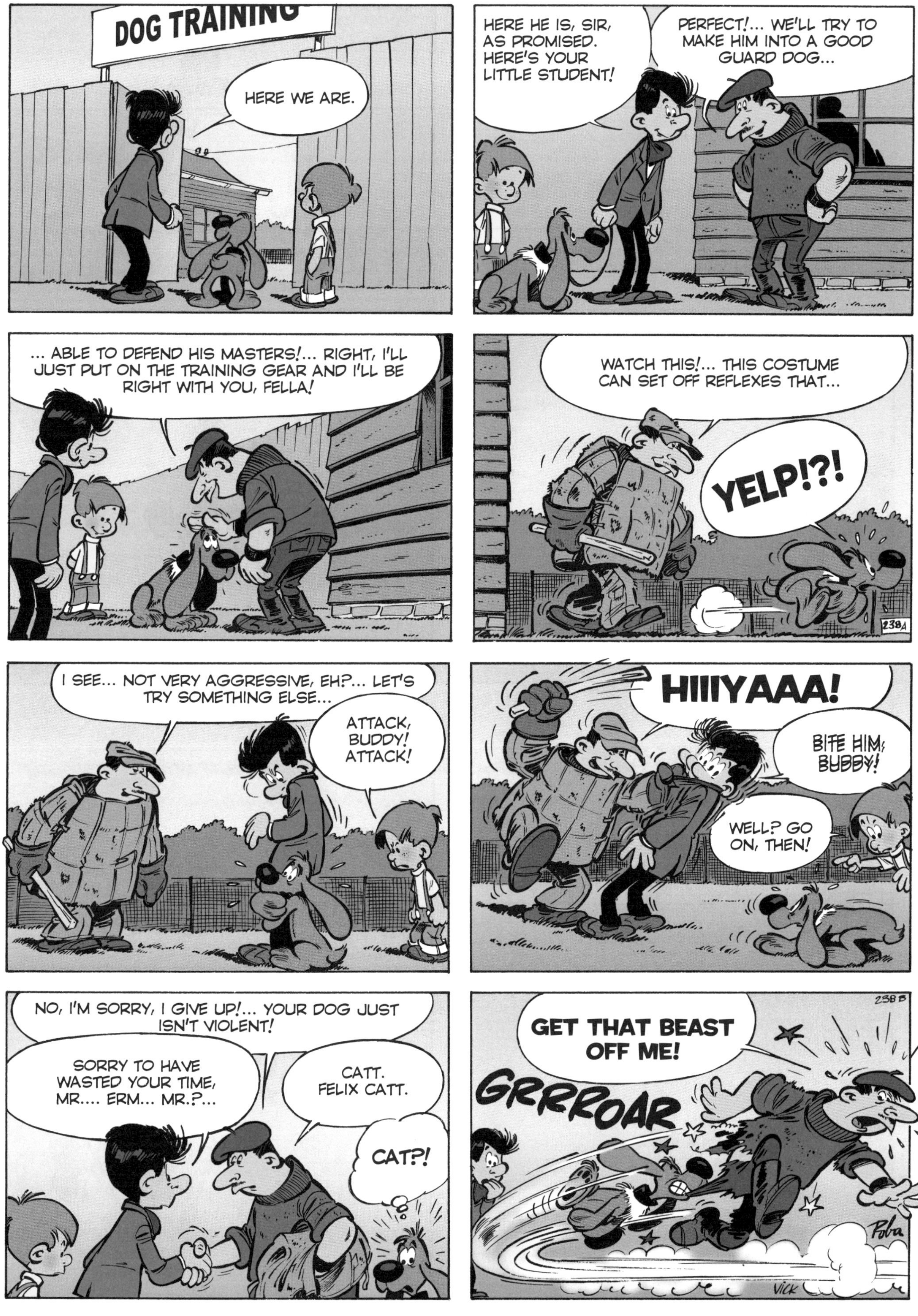

DOG TRAINING
HERE WE ARE.
HERE HE IS, SIR, AS PROMISED. HERE'S YOUR LITTLE STUDENT!
PERFECT!... WE'LL TRY TO MAKE HIM INTO A GOOD GUARD DOG...
... ABLE TO DEFEND HIS MASTERS!... RIGHT, I'LL JUST PUT ON THE TRAINING GEAR AND I'LL BE RIGHT WITH YOU, FELLA!
WATCH THIS!... THIS COSTUME CAN SET OFF REFLEXES THAT...
YELP!?!
I SEE... NOT VERY AGGRESSIVE, EH?... LET'S TRY SOMETHING ELSE...
ATTACK, BUDDY! ATTACK!
HIIIYAAA!
BITE HIM, BUDDY!
WELL? GO ON, THEN!
NO, I'M SORRY, I GIVE UP!... YOUR DOG JUST ISN'T VIOLENT!
SORRY TO HAVE WASTED YOUR TIME, MR.... ERM... MR.?...
CATT. FELIX CATT.
CAT?!
GET THAT BEAST OFF ME!
GRRROAR

Bone Meal

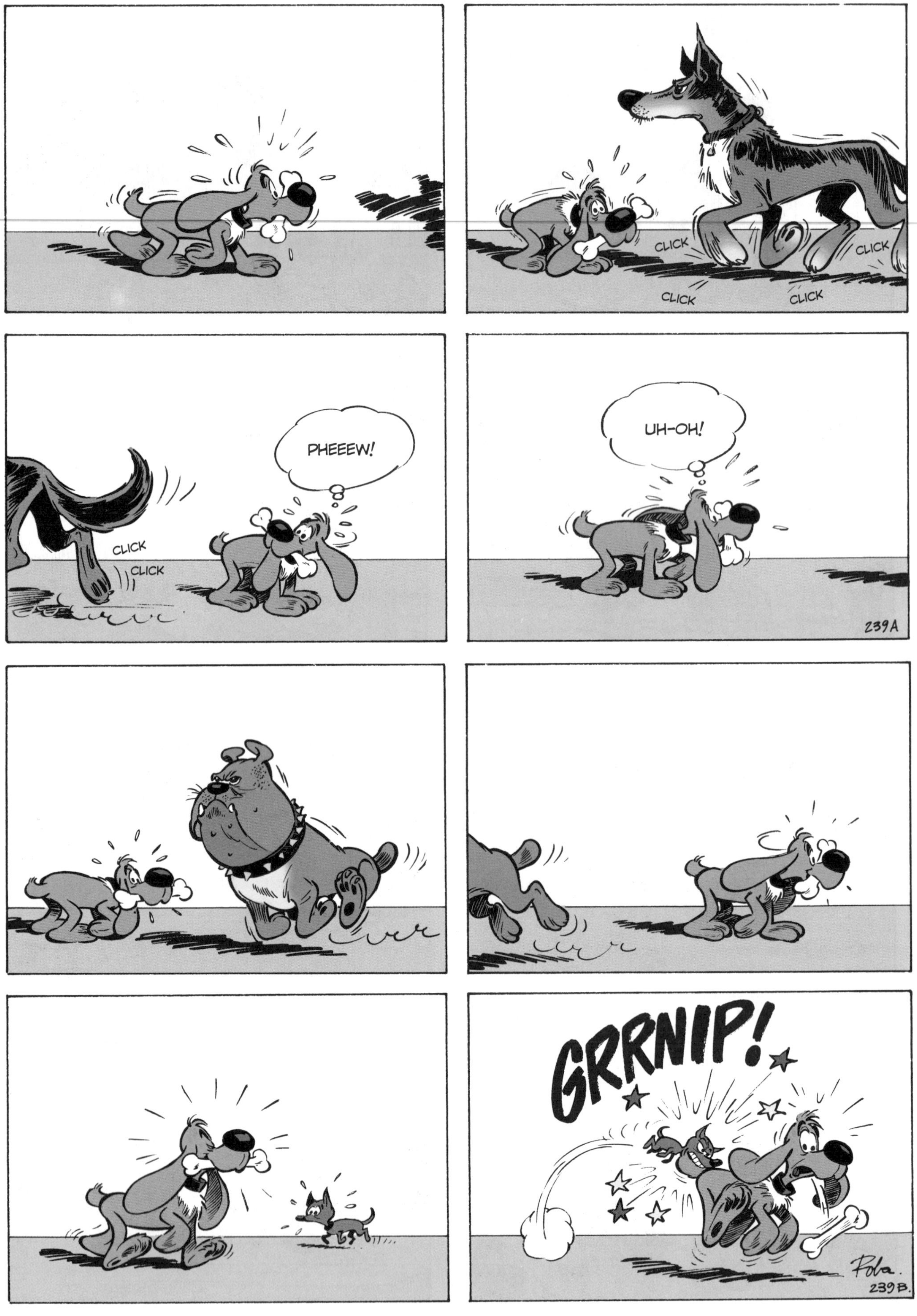
CLICK
CLICK
CLICK
CLICK
PHEEEW!
CLICK
CLICK
UH-OH!
239A
GRRNIP!
Roba.
239B.

Fit for a Ding

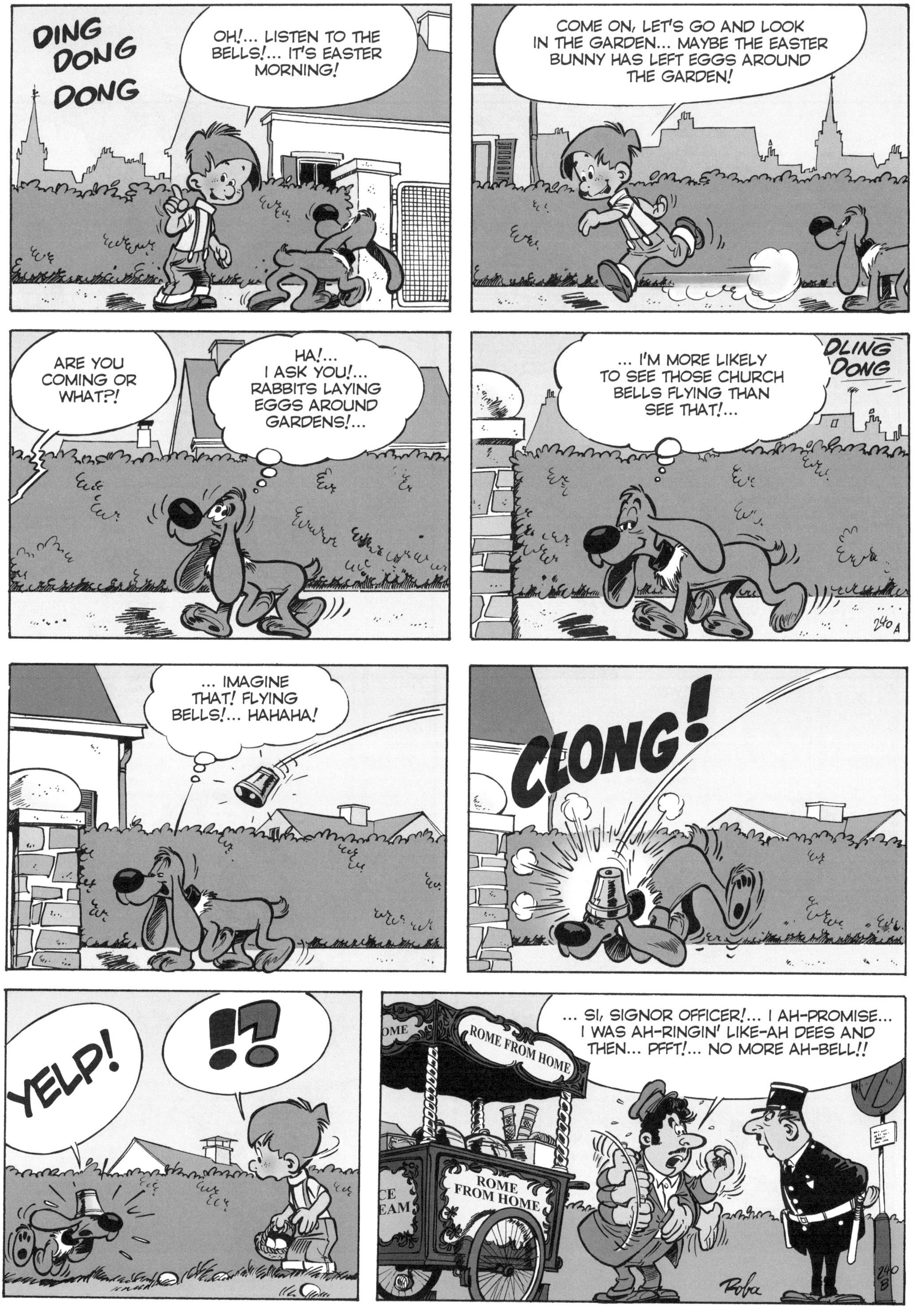
DING DONG DONG
OH!... LISTEN TO THE BELLS!... IT'S EASTER MORNING!
COME ON, LET'S GO AND LOOK IN THE GARDEN... MAYBE THE EASTER BUNNY HAS LEFT EGGS AROUND THE GARDEN!
ARE YOU COMING OR WHAT?!
HA!... I ASK YOU!... RABBITS LAYING EGGS AROUND GARDENS!...
... I'M MORE LIKELY TO SEE THOSE CHURCH BELLS FLYING THAN SEE THAT!...
DLING DONG
240 A
... IMAGINE THAT! FLYING BELLS!... HAHAHA!
CLONG!
YELP!
!?
ROME FROM HOME
ROME FROM HOME
... SI, SIGNOR OFFICER!... I AH-PROMISE... I WAS AH-RINGIN' LIKE-AH DEES AND THEN... PFFT!... NO MORE AH-BELL!!
Roba
240 B

Buddy and Gym

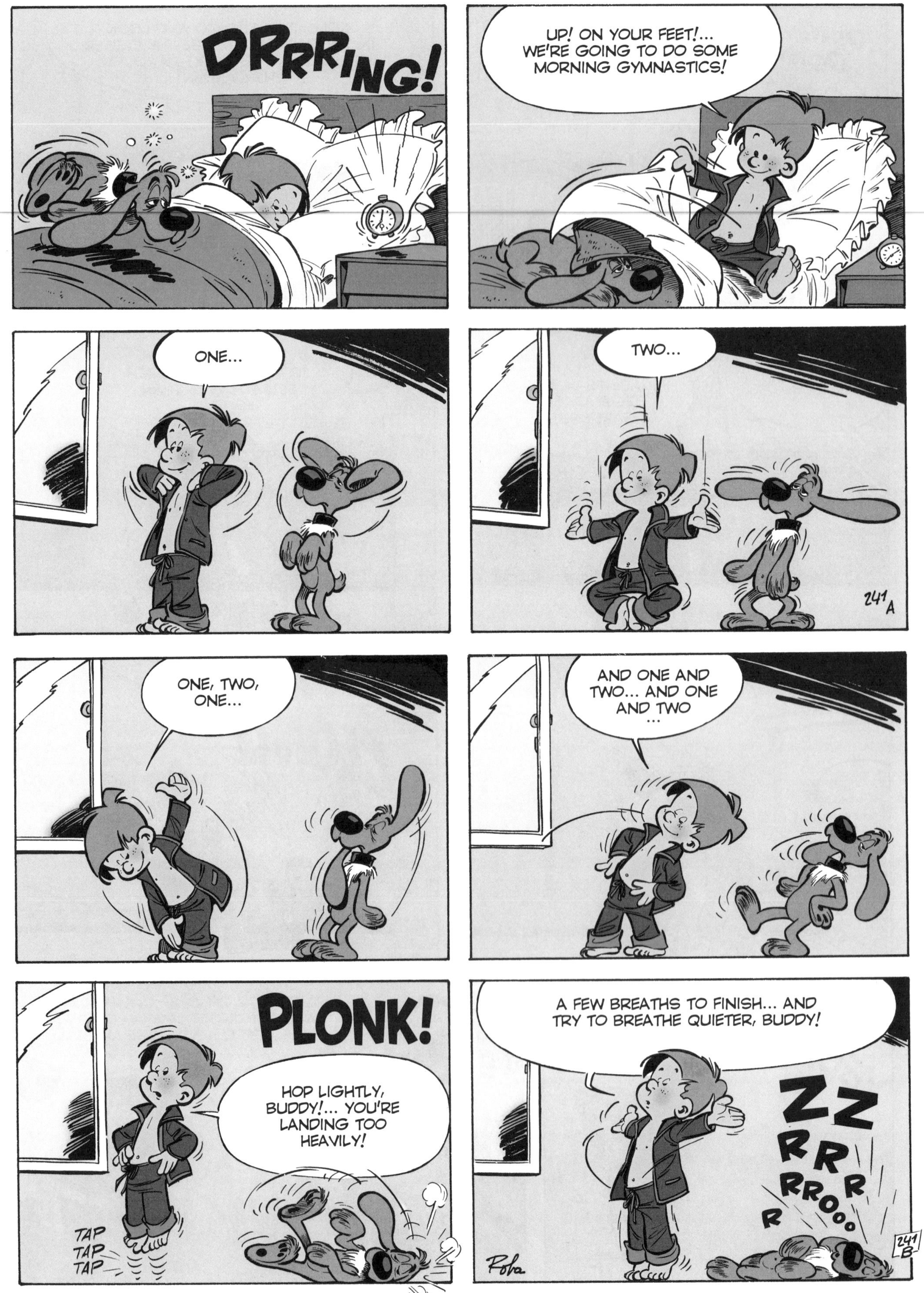
DRRRING!
UP! ON YOUR FEET!... WE'RE GOING TO DO SOME MORNING GYMNASTICS!
ONE...
TWO...
241 A
ONE, TWO, ONE...
AND ONE AND TWO... AND ONE AND TWO ...
PLONK!
HOP LIGHTLY, BUDDY!... YOU'RE LANDING TOO HEAVILY!
TAP TAP TAP
A FEW BREATHS TO FINISH... AND TRY TO BREATHE QUIETER, BUDDY!
ZZ RRR RRROOO R
Roba
241 B

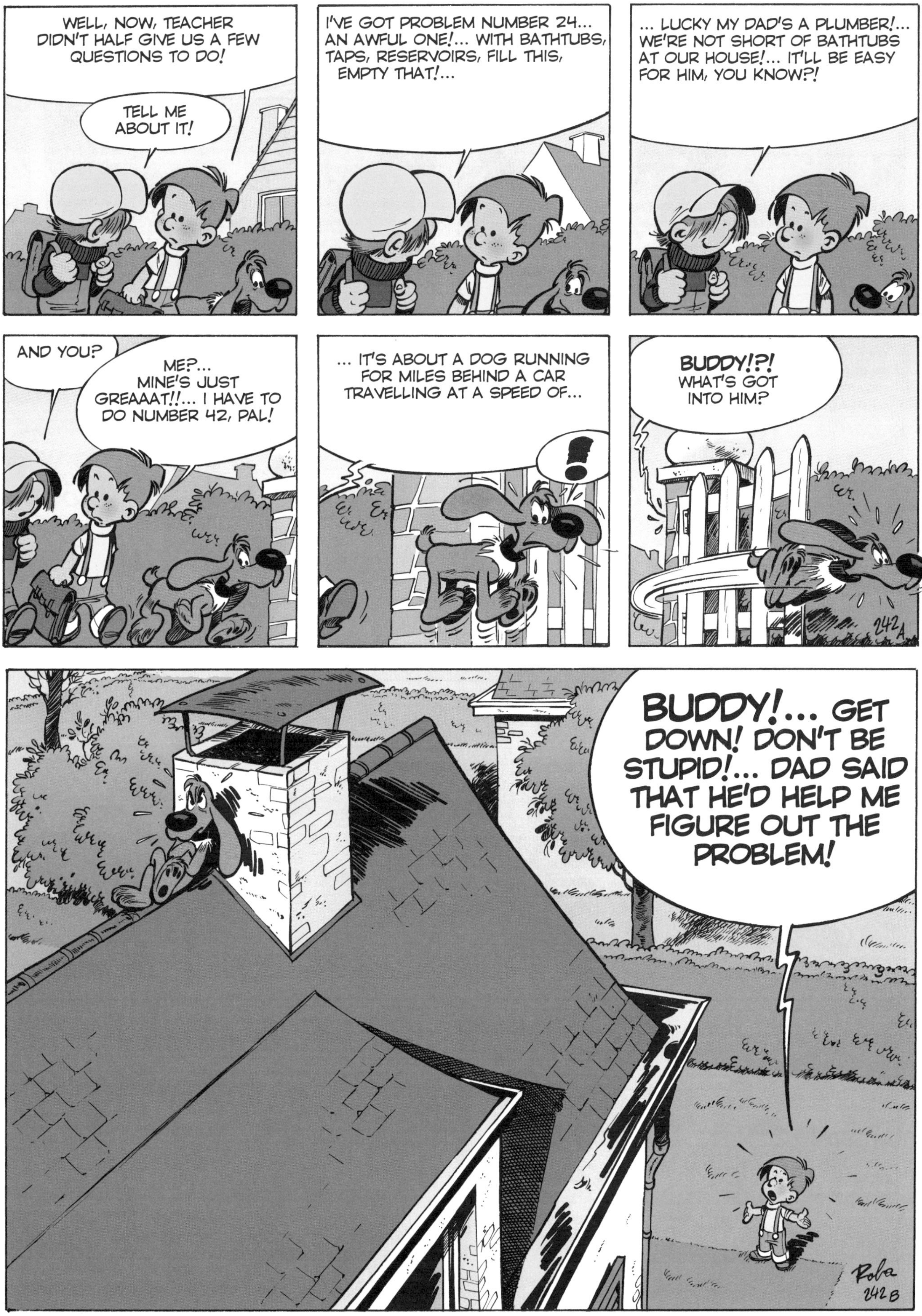
WELL, NOW, TEACHER DIDN'T HALF GIVE US A FEW QUESTIONS TO DO!
TELL ME ABOUT IT!
I'VE GOT PROBLEM NUMBER 24... AN AWFUL ONE!... WITH BATHTUBS, TAPS, RESERVOIRS, FILL THIS, EMPTY THAT!...
... LUCKY MY DAD'S A PLUMBER!... WE'RE NOT SHORT OF BATHTUBS AT OUR HOUSE!... IT'LL BE EASY FOR HIM, YOU KNOW?!
AND YOU?
ME?... MINE'S JUST GREAAAT!!... I HAVE TO DO NUMBER 42, PAL!
... IT'S ABOUT A DOG RUNNING FOR MILES BEHIND A CAR TRAVELLING AT A SPEED OF...
!
BUDDY!?! WHAT'S GOT INTO HIM?
242A
BUDDY!... GET DOWN! DON'T BE STUPID!... DAD SAID THAT HE'D HELP ME FIGURE OUT THE PROBLEM!
Roba
242B

Recipe for Disaster

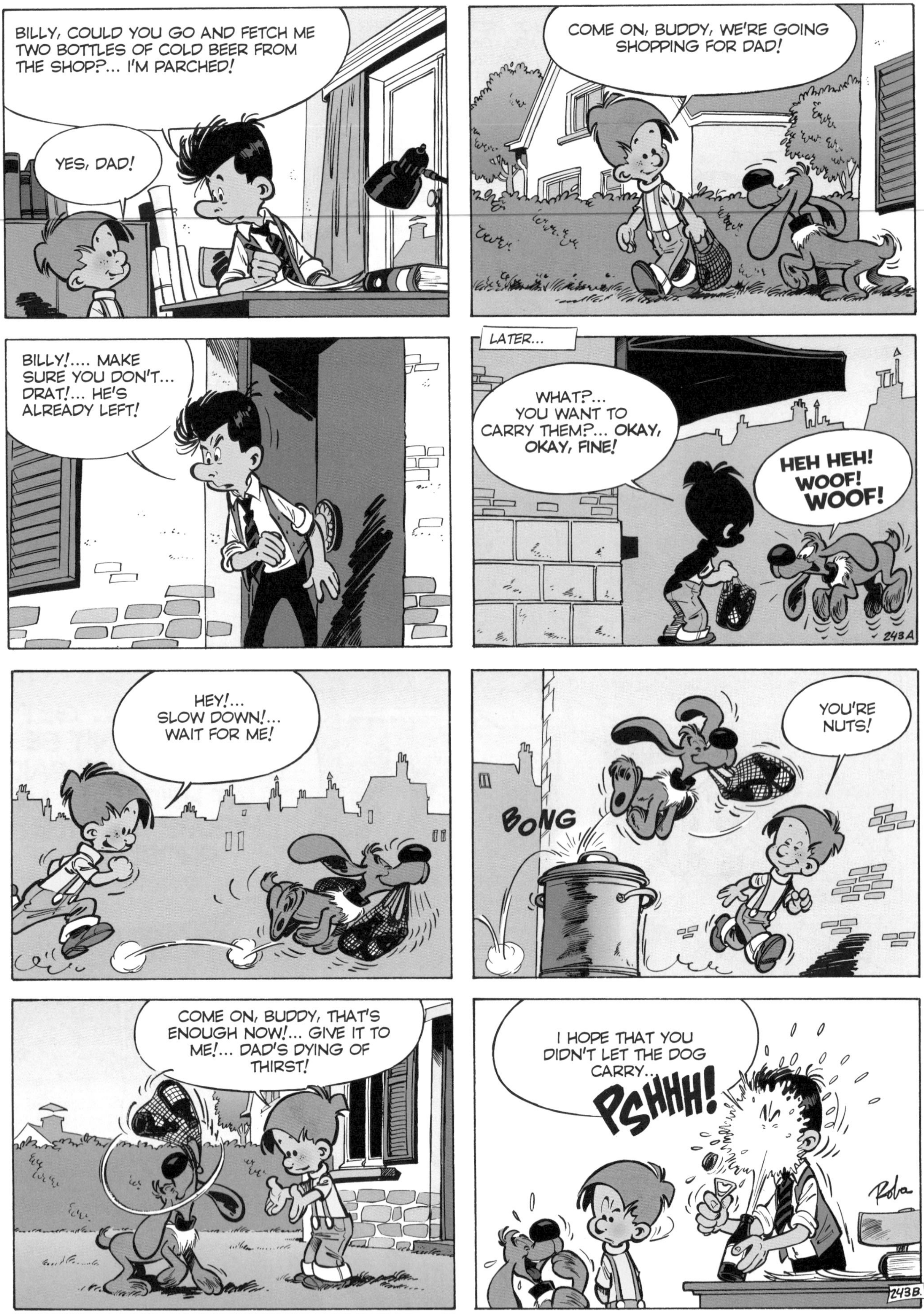
BILLY, COULD YOU GO AND FETCH ME TWO BOTTLES OF COLD BEER FROM THE SHOP?... I'M PARCHED!
YES, DAD!
COME ON, BUDDY, WE'RE GOING SHOPPING FOR DAD!
BILLY!.... MAKE SURE YOU DON'T... DRAT!... HE'S ALREADY LEFT!
LATER...
WHAT?... YOU WANT TO CARRY THEM?... OKAY, OKAY, FINE!
HEH HEH! WOOF! WOOF!
243 A
HEY!... SLOW DOWN!... WAIT FOR ME!
BONG
YOU'RE NUTS!
COME ON, BUDDY, THAT'S ENOUGH NOW!... GIVE IT TO ME!... DAD'S DYING OF THIRST!
I HOPE THAT YOU DIDN'T LET THE DOG CARRY...
PSHHH!
Roba
243 B.

Sweetness

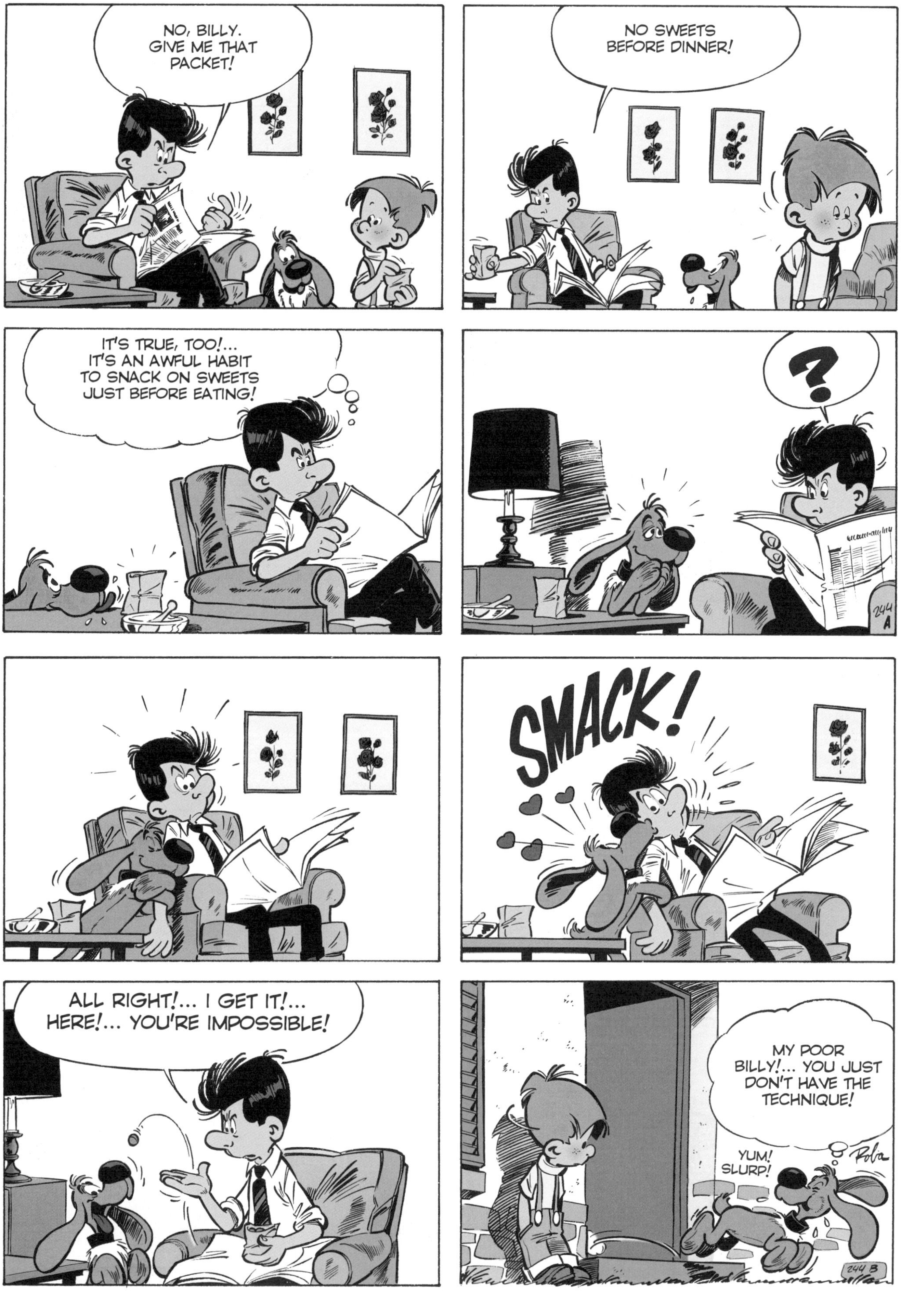
NO, BILLY. GIVE ME THAT PACKET!
NO SWEETS BEFORE DINNER!
IT'S TRUE, TOO!... IT'S AN AWFUL HABIT TO SNACK ON SWEETS JUST BEFORE EATING!
?
SMACK!
ALL RIGHT!... I GET IT!... HERE!... YOU'RE IMPOSSIBLE!
MY POOR BILLY!... YOU JUST DON'T HAVE THE TECHNIQUE!
YUM! SLURP!

The Naked Truth

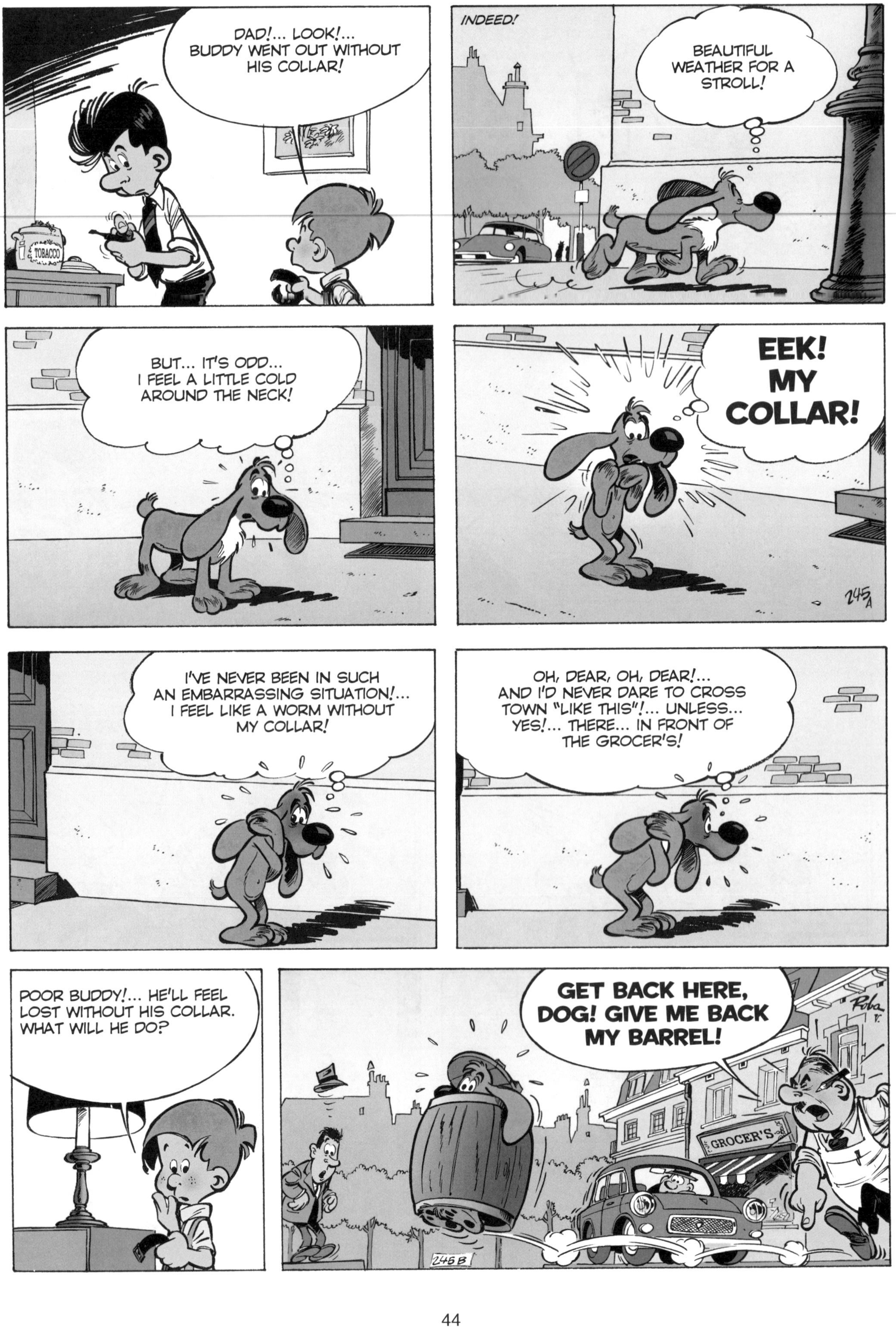
DAD!... LOOK!... BUDDY WENT OUT WITHOUT HIS COLLAR!
TOBACCO
INDEED!
BEAUTIFUL WEATHER FOR A STROLL!
BUT... IT'S ODD... I FEEL A LITTLE COLD AROUND THE NECK!
EEK! MY COLLAR!
245A
I'VE NEVER BEEN IN SUCH AN EMBARRASSING SITUATION!... I FEEL LIKE A WORM WITHOUT MY COLLAR!
OH, DEAR, OH, DEAR!... AND I'D NEVER DARE TO CROSS TOWN "LIKE THIS"!... UNLESS... YES!... THERE... IN FRONT OF THE GROCER'S!
POOR BUDDY!... HE'LL FEEL LOST WITHOUT HIS COLLAR. WHAT WILL HE DO?
GET BACK HERE, DOG! GIVE ME BACK MY BARREL!
GROCER'S
245B
Roba

Mirror, mirror, on the Floor...

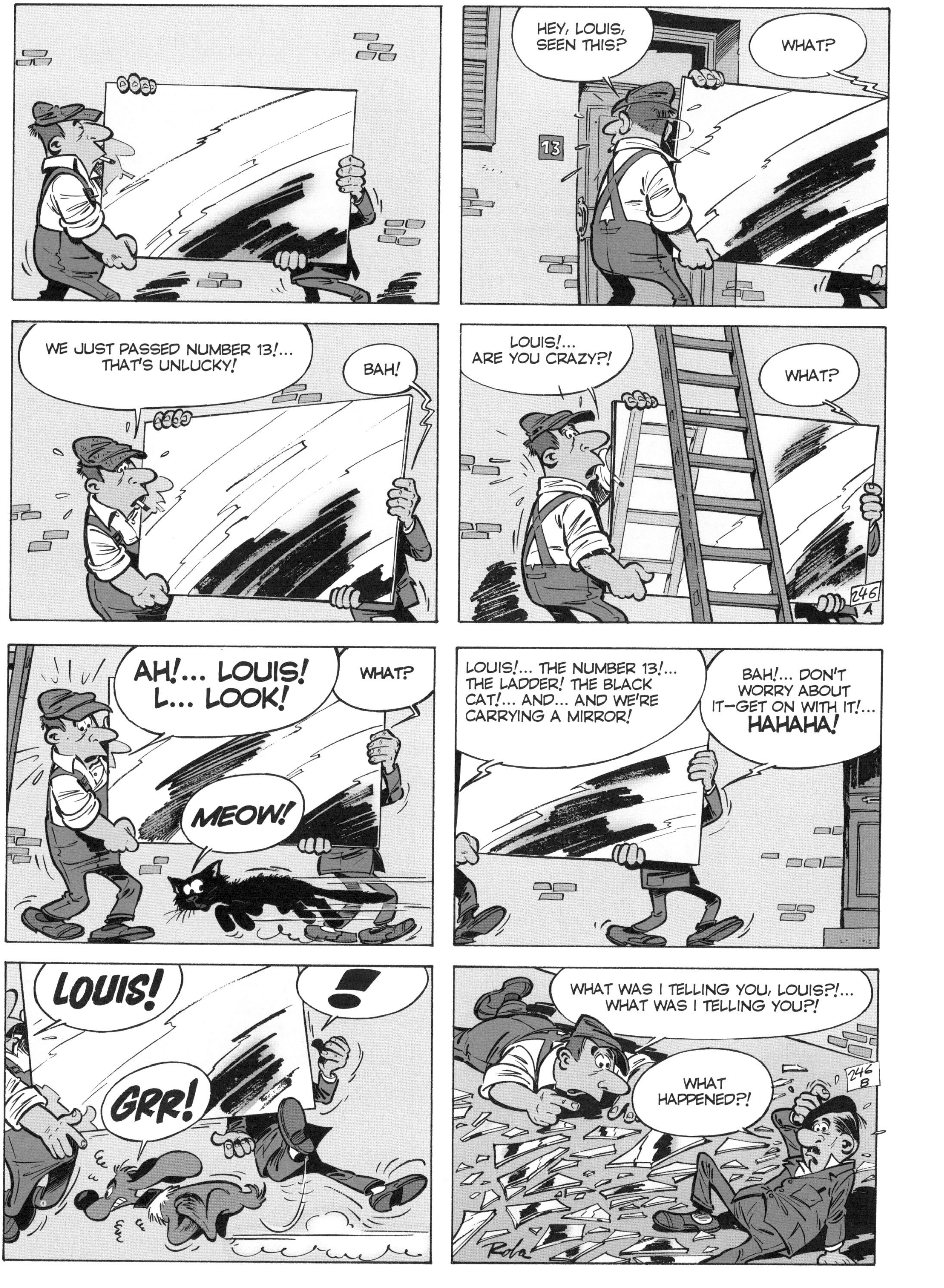

HEY, LOUIS, SEEN THIS?
WHAT?
13
WE JUST PASSED NUMBER 13!... THAT'S UNLUCKY!
BAH!
LOUIS!... ARE YOU CRAZY?!
WHAT?
246 A
AH!... LOUIS! L... LOOK!
WHAT?
MEOW!
LOUIS!... THE NUMBER 13!... THE LADDER! THE BLACK CAT!... AND... AND WE'RE CARRYING A MIRROR!
BAH!... DON'T WORRY ABOUT IT—GET ON WITH IT!... HAHAHA!
LOUIS!
!
GRR!
WHAT WAS I TELLING YOU, LOUIS?!... WHAT WAS I TELLING YOU?!
WHAT HAPPENED?!
246 B
Roba

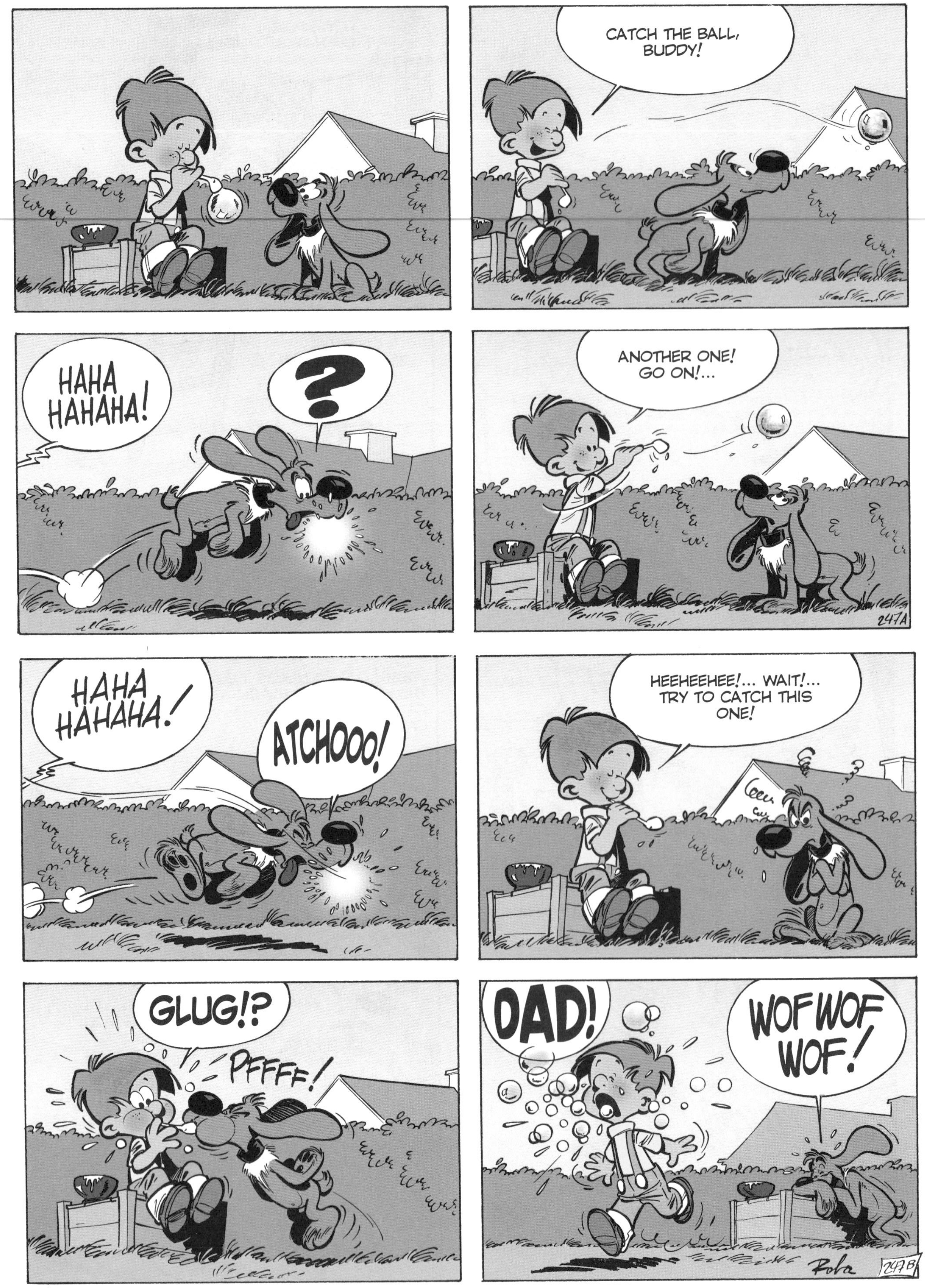
CATCH THE BALL, BUDDY!
HAHA HAHAHA!
?
ANOTHER ONE! GO ON!...
247A
HAHA HAHAHA!
ATCHOOO!
HEEHEEHEE!... WAIT!... TRY TO CATCH THIS ONE!
GLUG!?
PFFFF!
DAD!
WOF WOF WOF!
Roba
247B

Police Crackdown

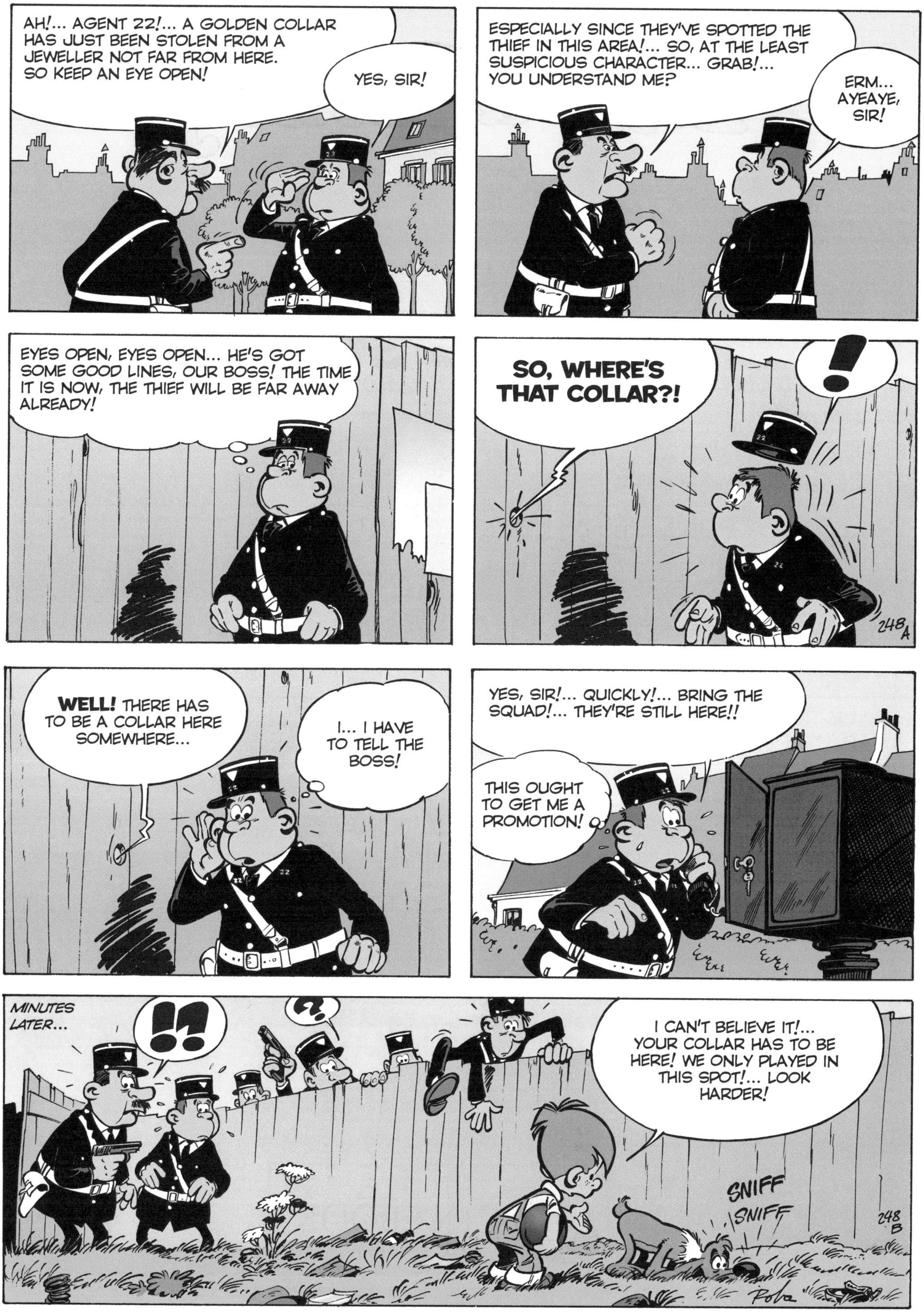

AH!... AGENT 22!... A GOLDEN COLLAR HAS JUST BEEN STOLEN FROM A JEWELLER NOT FAR FROM HERE. SO KEEP AN EYE OPEN!
YES, SIR!
ESPECIALLY SINCE THEY'VE SPOTTED THE THIEF IN THIS AREA!... SO, AT THE LEAST SUSPICIOUS CHARACTER... GRAB!... YOU UNDERSTAND ME?
ERM... AYEAYE, SIR!
EYES OPEN, EYES OPEN... HE'S GOT SOME GOOD LINES, OUR BOSS! THE TIME IT IS NOW, THE THIEF WILL BE FAR AWAY ALREADY!
SO, WHERE'S THAT COLLAR?!
!
248 A
WELL! THERE HAS TO BE A COLLAR HERE SOMEWHERE...
I... I HAVE TO TELL THE BOSS!
YES, SIR!... QUICKLY!... BRING THE SQUAD!... THEY'RE STILL HERE!!
THIS OUGHT TO GET ME A PROMOTION!
MINUTES LATER...
!!
?
I CAN'T BELIEVE IT!... YOUR COLLAR HAS TO BE HERE! WE ONLY PLAYED IN THIS SPOT!... LOOK HARDER!
SNIFF
SNIFF
248 B
Roba

Billy & Buddy

COMING SOON

2
Roba
Billy & Buddy
BORED SILLY
WITH BILLY
CINEBOOK
The 9th Art Publisher

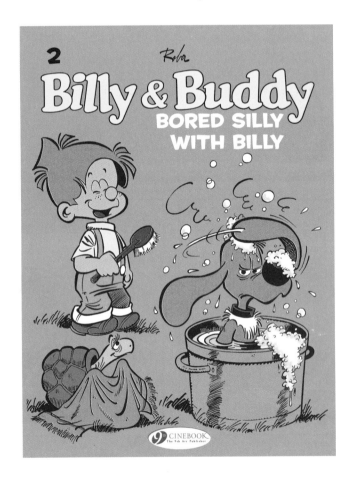

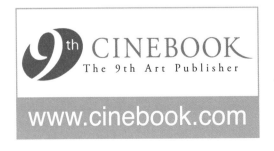